NOT NICE

Other books by Neil S. Reddy published by Dank House Manor

Hound of the Biscuit Barrel

Giles Bastet 9th Heavenly Cat

Jubjub Juice

Bottle vs Avalon

Byron Beyond the Firmament

NOT NICE

By

Neil S. Reddy

NOT NICE

Neil S. Reddy

ISBN 978-1-0676056-0-5

Cover Illustration by Ian Parker

Dank House Manor Publications 2026

ACKNOWLEDGMENTS

This is a work of fiction containing historical figures any resemblance to any living person is entirely coincidental.

For the feral, you know who you are ...

There was a little girl,
Who had a little curl,
Right in the middle of her forehead.
When she was good,
She was very good indeed,
But when she was bad she was horrid.

Henry Wadsworth Longfellow

NOT NICE

1

A beast roams our housing estate at night. I first saw it as a child from my bedroom window. It was a monstrous rhinoceros, a heaving mismatch of angles and armoured bulk, glowing like a nightmare unicorn in the light of a March blood moon. It was an ugliness that had no place in the world of men. I saw it and it saw me, and it knew me as one of its own.

My name is Anne Marie Codner, not 'Anna-Conda' or 'Anna-Conda the Beast of Basingstoke,' as I was once called. My name was a gift horse to schoolyard bullies. An easy taunt, because I am ugly. I know it. I see the truth when I look in the mirror. I've been disguising the truth since I was eleven years old. There I'd stand, in front of the mirror, slapping on the face the world calls 'girl.' I use foundation and blusher to hide the crypt pale pallor, lipstick to reshape the thin-lipped sneer, eyeliner to enlarge my snake sharp eyes, and shading to create contours to hide the dagger sharp lines. My eyebrows I never touch, I have perfect eyebrows – job done, face on, out into the world I go. And how does the world greet me? With catcalls and demands:

“Wrap yourself around this Anna-Conda.”

“Go on give us a smile,”

“Smile it suits your face,”

“Go on give us a smile, it might never happen,”

“Smile it can’t be that bad.”

And so I smile, even though it is that bad, and it did happen, I happened. But it seems a smile and a bit of make-up is all it takes to convince some people that I’m okay, that I’m safe; or perhaps nobody’s really paying attention. I’m paying attention. I am present. I find myself fascinating. I can see the curl of the burl beneath the veneer, the dead-eyed serpent glaring behind the eyes. I think mother must have seen it too, perhaps she heard the hiss beneath the gurgle when I was laying in my crib. I was nine months old when she tried to smother me.

My maleficence formed in her womb. Her body knew and tried to abort me several times. Pregnancy was not a blissful for my mother, she had a hard time or so I’m told, “a hard time of it,” is all my father ever said, and as mother was herself an only child whose parents died young, I had no one else to tell me otherwise. I suspect she had an inkling of the evil growing within her but once I was there, once she held my little reptilian face in her arms, there was no denying it. I respect her for trying to do something about it. The intercession of a Blue Nun saved my life. A bottle of Blue

Nun wielded by my father, cracked across the back of my mother's head as she tried to smother me in the crib. Mother was taken away, given seventeen stitches, and the help others perceived she needed. She returned almost a year later, utterly broken. Withdrawn and silent, her presence a permanent absence our house, until she finally exited six years later via a barbiturate overdose. Her departure had as much impact on me as her presence, I cannot say the same for my father.

Father began drinking before the funeral service started, and apart from a brief "Gladys" induced dry spell – I'll get to that later - I don't think he ever stopped. But I won't use my father's frailties as an excuse for my actions, I insist they have no bearing on who I am. The spectre of child abuse has no place in my story – yes, like every other girl of my generation, and I'm sure of every generation there's ever been, I have been exposed to the gropers, dick swingers and vampire leers of men. But my father was not amongst them. You would not believe how many psychiatrists, psychologists and therapists have disputed my father's behaviour, and when I insist the man was not a rapist how many have smiled, cocked their heads and condescendingly said; "are you sure? Could it be that the memory is too painful to admit to?" Only a man would suggest something was too painful for a woman. My father was a decent man, settling down to a decent life, when a cluster-fuck bomb dropped into his lap – mental illness, suicide and a serpent girl child that terrified him. Is it any wonder he drank? I was never molested, beaten or raped by my father. And I never went hungry. If our relationship lacked affection, it's because I never sought it, and I certainly never gave my father any reason to think he was anything other than a stranger to me. He did what I required. He paid the bills, signed the forms, fetched Tampax from the corner store when I asked him to, and kept out of my way – and still he managed to irritate me. There were times I wanted to watch him choke on his own blood, but I don't hold him responsible for what I became. I am my own creation.

My infancy was plagued by night-terrors, which still occasionally arise in times of psychic stress or physical illness. My terrors took many forms - faces moving in the curtains, witches reaching for me from the wallpaper, or I'd find myself clinging to the window ledge of an impossibly large tower, with rats nipping at my fingertips - but the most often repeated dream went like this;

it's nighttime, I'm climbing down a steep stone staircase with a group of grey faced old women. We're all wearing the same drab grey ill-fitting nighties, and no shoes, we're all very frightened. The steps are narrow and the blackness beyond them endless. I could fall at any moment, and then a stone face appears in the wall blocking our path. It asks each old lady in turn a question, and when they fail to answer, as all do, it eats them up and then vomits up a stream of chewed flesh and blood. This filth makes the steps even more treacherous, and I'm sure I'm going to slip, but I keep walking in line, terrified, knowing my time will come. And then I recognise the face in the wall, it's me –

I once told a therapist that dream, and he mansplained that;

"The Freudian interpretation of dreams is a discredited and obsolete intervention with no therapeutic value. Dreams occur when your sleeping mind sorts through unwanted images and thoughts, trying to forget useless information, and sometimes those images coalesce to form the frightening scenarios we call bad dreams. But I'll tell you this for nothing, you think bad things, and you'll dream bad things, it's as simple as that."

What an arsehole; and what a moribund view of the world – Lego thinking builds Lego worlds.

If Freud or one of his anally retentive disciples had known about my childhood preoccupations with sex they would have had a field day. A preternaturally sexually curious female with night terrors and homicidal tendencies – Freud would have been all over me, dirty old man. My curiosity in all things biological, first drew the attention of the authorities when I was five. My teacher, Ms Dobbs, a diminutive woman that resembled a Weeble – Weebles Wobble (But They Don't Fall Down) - in purple slacks, caught me playing doctors and nurses with two other little girls in the primary school's Wendy House. All the mothers were called to the school to address the situation, and as I'd chosen to be the doctor, I was singled out as the ringleader – which in all fairness, I was. I can still see my medicated mother's response to the gathered parental outrage; glazed, distant and yet crushed. I promised her I would never do it again. I wanted to be good, although I failed to see what I had done wrong. Six weeks later the headmistress called my mother again, this time I'd been caught in the Wendy House with two compliant little boys. I had changed my ways, but somehow, I was still wrong, it didn't seem fair. Again, I promised I would never do it again. It has been conjectured, or should I say a theory has been presented to me, that suggests this scenario is evidence that I have sublimated frightening sexual thoughts and urges into a need to control others, which has thereafter become my primary form of sexual gratification – can you believe they actually pay people to say this nonsense? Is it any wonder mental health services are in the state they're in?

On my seventh birthday, Mother tried to organise a party for me. Given her chemically induced vacancy, I can't say how committed she was to this, but come the day, she'd had no confirmations and no bugger turned up. Perhaps my sexual exploits had made me a social pariah. As compensation, father took me for a day out at a castle; Mother couldn't face the prospect and stayed home. I didn't mind seeing castles because that's where knights and unicorns and exciting stuff with spinning-wheels happened. Although this castle didn't have unicorns, it was the place some king or other had been murdered; that at least sounded mildly intriguing. I remember asking the guide, how the king had been murdered, he blushed and looked to my father who replied. "If she's old enough to ask, she's old enough to know."

The attendant couldn't meet my eye as he intoned, "they held him down with a table and forced a red-hot poker up his…back passage. They say his screams were heard for miles around."

My reply: "I should bloody think so too," solicited a wave of laughter and curious looks that still warm me to this day.

I must have fallen asleep in the car on the way home, as I have no memory of getting there or getting into bed, but what happened next, I'll never forget. I awoke in the early hours to the huff, huff, huffing of a steam-train beneath my window. I stood on my bed and looked out onto our front garden, and there I saw a monster unicorn with glassy red metal skin, looking up at me, as paving stones split beneath its feet. I dropped to my knees and hid beneath the covers and waited for night to pass. Father woke me the next morning and announced that Mother had died. I asked how? And as I was old enough to ask, I was old enough to be told – "your mummy wasn't well, she took pills to make her better, but last night she took too many and fell asleep and drifted away." He went on to assure me that she felt no pain, but all I could imagine was a silent scream that nobody heard as she felt herself falling into darkness. Gone, and I barely noticed she was there. That night I dreamed the blood unicorn carried her away on its back to a better place, a place without me.

Four weeks later, I stood next to father in a crematorium that had all the warmth of a public toilet; throttling a bunch of wilting flowers, as a man in a black dress got up and talked about a woman, he admitted he'd never met. The woman he'd never met sounded very nice, a lot of fun, but I had no idea who he was talking about. And then I realised he was talking about my mother. I felt cheated, and that made me feel angry. I threw my flowers at the man in the black dress for making me angry. He coughed, buried his face in his stupid book, and asked us to bow our heads and pray. Father cried, and I had a terrible longing for a chocolate drizzled banana split – I guess I'd moved on.

My behaviour certainly took a leap into the shadows after mother's death; I won't deny it. Acting out, is what psychologists call it, I called it having fun. Let me give you an example; the Ekal Event.

Peanut butter was banned from my class because Raymond Ekal, had a nut allergy, which was a rather unusual occurrence back then, and such things weren't as readily accommodated as I hear they are today - back then you paid your money and took your chances. Now it just so happened that I liked peanut butter, it was one food source I could access whenever father was late home from work or too drunk to grill fish fingers. So, when we were asked not to bring peanut butter into class, my nose was put-out. Raymond Ekal was making me go hungry. Being the child of a one parent family, I was entitled to a free school meal, but a combination of factors, such as:

A) Having to queue in the 'Free School Meals' line, with other 'benefit kids.'

B) The way the stuff was slopped out – 'slopping out' being prison slang for the morning routine of emptying the piss-pots – which says all you need to know about the actual food.
Made the experience, distasteful and humiliating to me. Therefore, in order to avoid these humiliations, I brought peanut butter sandwiches to school, and I didn't see why I should stop. And so, one morning before school I smeared a length of tinfoil with peanut butter, folded it up and put it in my coat pocket. During class I requested a toilet break and went straight to my coat hanger and then to Raymon's bag, where I located his lunchbox - a nightmare of wholemeal, fruity goodness - and transferred the smear of peanut butter to the centre of Raymond's cheese and lettuce sandwich. When lunchtime came, I made sure I had a good view.

First bite of the sandwich – and all's well - followed by a drink of water – and all's well - second bite – still nothing – did this mean Raymond was a faker? Then another sip of water followed by another bite of the sandwich and BAM! Little Raymond's on his feet, emitting a high-pitched screech that set everyone's teeth on edge. His face turned bright red and then blue, and then he's rolling on the floor in a blind panic. Luckily for Raymond one of the dinner ladies, Edna, a neighbour of ours with oak tree ankles, knew what she was about. She picked blue-faced Raymond up by the scruff of the neck, threw him over her shoulder and rushed him out of the hall. Soon after an ambulance arrived and whisked Raymond off to hospital. Edna got a mention in the local paper, and all the parents got another letter reminding them, not to send their children to school with peanut butter. So, no real harm done.

My father read the letter with a weary and hungover eye, "do you know anything about this?"

"I know Raymond, he's small and smells of wee."

"That's not a nice thing to say Anne Marie, you shouldn't say things like that," father scowled.

"Sorry…he's small and smells of urine," I scowled back, "better?"

"Don't talk to me like that young lady," he fumed, "you know exactly what I mean, did you have anything to do with this?"

"With what?"

"This incident at school! This boy Raymond. Did you have anything to do with it?"

“I saw it happen. His faced turned blue and I think he urined himself.”

Father’s solution was predictably reactionary; “you need to get out more. Make friends.”

“Why? To what purpose?”

“I don’t know, to have some fun, get some exercise… learn some social skills.”

What he really meant was “to get you out of my hair.”

“What about sports? Netball or...” he seemed to have reached the limit of his ‘girl sport’ knowledge, “...there’s always ballet?”

“Me in a tutu! I think not. People will laugh.”

“Why would people laugh?”

“Because I’d look ridiculous and people are horrible.”

Thankfully football had yet to be aimed at a female fanbase, so I wasn’t obliged to fake interest in that nonsense. At school the options were gym, netball or hockey. All shared the same drawback, cold legs and a sweaty fanny thanks to the regulation reinforced gusset of nuclear blast proof gym knickers. Hockey involved swinging a deadly weapon, which sounded like fun, but it turned out you weren't allowed to play hockey until you reached secondary or senior school – when raging hormones meant death blows were much less likely to occur. As that wasn't an immediate option, I did consider table tennis, but "ping-pong" – ping-pongers hate it when you call it that - would only be fun if they let you batter your opponent and not the ball, and that's definitely against the rules. As father wasn't going to backdown I had to approach the problem in a practical manner and decided to make a list of pros and cons in my ledger, but what I ended up with was a cons and cons list, based on requirements and risk.

Socially Acceptable Sporting Activities Providing Opportunities for Social Integration & the Resources Required to Socially Integrate.	Formulation: Negative Aspect of Sporting Activity (N= Normal, H= High, VH = Very High, A= Absolute)
Gym: essential need = gym + crutch crushing leotard.	Early morning start A + Being eyed up by perverts VH + Being felt up by perverts VH + Chance of rape - H.

Horse riding essentials = horse + stables + hay + boots and hat + money for vets and farriers.	Early mornings - A Being eyed-up by horsey pervert - VH Being felt up by horsey perverts - H Chance of rape by horsey people - H. Pity, I don't mind horses, horses are ok.
Track & field essentials = track & field + money for equipment.	Early morning starts - A Cold early morning starts - A Being eyed-up by perverts - H Risk of molestation - N Chance of rape - N.
Swimming essentials = swimming pool + non-see-through leotard.	Basically naked whilst dunking self in other people's piss & eye stinging chemicals - A Early mornings - A Being eyed-up by perverts - A + Risk of molestation - VH Chance of rape - AA
Tennis essentials = tennis court – white gym	Early mornings - H

knickers – tennis stuff – balls.	Being eyed-up by perverts - AA Risk of molestation - H Chance of rape – N but you've got to mix with total wankers and spoilt brats.

I presented my calculations to father, and although at first disturbed, he did agree not to push me towards the indignities of netball and swimming etc, but I had to agree to give less sporty organised activities "a fair shake," … whatever that means.

I started with the Brownies, the paramilitary wing of the Girl Guides. I decided to aim for the Home Nurse badge, but when I brought in a dead squirrel, they immediately confiscated it and asked me to leave. Home Nurse badge didn't require the skill to dissect, and taxidermy was not a badge they were willing to support. Then came the Girls Brigade, the female child soldiers of Protestant Christendom. I could have done without the singing, but I rather liked the blue shirts and the marching up and down. There was something about its gently authoritarian approach I found very comforting. Sadly, I was thrown out of the local troop for cheering as the names on the War Memorial were readout on Remembrance Day. No one told me gratitude and appreciation had to be silent.

I thought I'd hit gold when I discovered an adventure playground had opened on the adjoining estate. It was a large square of waste ground surrounded by a twelve-foot wooden fence. You paid a quid for the day, and they gave you a pile of wood, a tin of nails and a hammer. I arrived when it opened at nine in the morning and by two o'clock, I'd built a rudimentary but functional trebuchet. I loaded up the firing arm with a bucket of flint and fired a volley over the fence. It seems I'd grossly underestimated the things power, but was spot-on when it came to trajectory, as I heard at least three windows smash. At four o'clock council officials arrived and closed the whole operation down.

Father was a little put-out that I'd run through (and closed) the estates limited offerings in less than three months, and threatened to inflict ballroom dancing on me…

Ballroom Dancing: ballroom – ridiculous dresses, tight shoes.	Ridiculous dresses + make-up + being felt up as standard + being molested by boy in public + public derision + loss of all self-esteem VVH

… but luckily, the very next day, I saw a poorly photocopied poster in the local shop window saying;

KARATE CLUB – WEDNESDAY NIGHT.

All Welcome. First Session Free.

Father was hesitant at first, I suspect he saw garnishing my violent disposition with assassin skills as a recipe for litigation. But he soon bought into the "martial arts are about self-control" vibe when he heard the sessions were held in the small community hall attached to our local pub. He walked me to every session twice a week for six months.

I loved karate, from the very first coordinated warm up, to the last group bow, I loved it all. I felt a deep heat rising within me every time I heard the snap of the heavy linen that came with a well-executed kick. My heart was warmed by the guttural Kiai battle cry, and I found peace in the power of control. However, karate did provide me with my first experience of inappropriate male attention that I can remember. I'd been paired off with a boy two years my senior. We were running through a repeating series of controlled blocks and punches, as we did every week; when he stepped forward, ran his hand over my chest, sneered and then stepped back; resuming his stance as if nothing had happened. I was frozen in a brain halting fog of shock and shame. I genuinely couldn't move – and then came the traitorous thought; "had I done something wrong?" I was ten, and as flat as a pancake in the chest department, but I knew what had just happened - he hadn't just touched me, he had copped a feel. And he did it because he thought he had the right to do it and would get away with it. And if I didn't do something – I'd be confirming his self-serving idiocy. The shame boiled into rage as I took up the stance for the next series of blocks.

As he stepped forward telegraphing his next swing, I stepped in too close, planted my feet firmly onto the mat, and extended my arm upwards with a sharp snap. The base of my palm connected with the tip of his nose. Blood gushed, splattering his tunic and trousers. He shrieked, fell to his knees, and wept. I stepped back, grinned, straightened the front of my keikogi, and checked it for stains – there were none, it was pristine.

"What happened?" the Sensei (a hairy welder named Burt from the nearby forklift factory) asked.

"He didn't block me," I replied with a shrug. The boy was too busy choking on his tears to protest; conclusion - accidents happen.

I shall forever be grateful to karate, for teaching me the benefits of regular, focused, disciplined exercise, and for introducing me to Horse-Faced Sally.

Sally Kent had her own set of catcalls to deal with:

"Hi Sally, why the long face?" – hearty ha.

"Saddle-up and ride my Sally," – hearty ha ha.

"Come on Sally, give us a smile, what about a kiss? A sugar cube for a kiss Sally?" – hearty ha ha ha.

"You're not upset are you Horse-Faced Sally Kent – neigh it isn't so." – HA! HA! HA!

Sally was a good person, but that was unimportant because Sally Kent looked like a horse. Her voice was an adenoidal creak that made cats run for cover, and her screeching laugh could dry your teeth at a hundred yards. Sadly, like all those who believe their appearance belies the true goodness of their soul; she was desperate to prove that beneath that horsey exterior and tooth drying laugh, she harboured a beautiful spirit. This and the worlds insensitivity to Sally's feelings, made her vulnerable to my dark proclivities. Talk about low hanging fruit.

I'd been attending the karate club for about six weeks when Sally offered to help me through my first Kata. The offer was innocently made, but I, being a corrupting bacillus, saw her kindness as an opportunity for devilment. Poor sweet Sally Kent, Karate aside, I don't think anybody had ever tried any moves on Sally before I came along. Boys were physically repulsed by her, and to be honest, most girls could do better. But I saw what I needed, someone vulnerable, obliging and in need of validation. Sally would pop-round two or three times a week after school, and we'd run through the Kata in the kitchen for about half an hour. Sally was a very good teacher, so by the third week I was move perfect, smooth, controlled and with just the right amount of snap. We always had tea and biscuits in the front room after our sessions, but after successfully running through the Kata, I invited her to go upstairs and see my bedroom. Once there, I used the same move on Sally that got karate-boy his broken nose, and although Sally was shocked, she was not unresponsive. Thereafter her "helping with the Kata" visits shifted to "helping with the homework" visits and permanently decamped to my bedroom. Father was good enough to slip her five quid per session – making her richer and happier, in more ways than one.

Once again, for the record, I'm not looking to hold anybody but myself to account here, but I do feel this is one of the few occasions when circumstance dictated the ends. I was a vicious little devil with a fascination for knots –

honestly there was nothing the Girl Guides could teach me – and Sally was lonely, and in need of some appreciation and attention. I gave her both – at least twice a week, with added lessons in knottology. Our conjoining lasted two years, and then at the age of fourteen, just as the spokes of my menstrual cycle finally began to spin, I quite suddenly lost all interest in sex. That's right, just as my compatriots were becoming obsessed with all things sweaty, firm and boyish, I became a priggish, uptight little prude. Sally, now sixteen, was heartbroken, and out of pocket, but I had to follow my heart. I always liked a little bit of pain with my pleasure – as long as the pain was someone else's, but what I wanted, what I needed, was more than I was willing to take from dear sweet Horse-Faced Sally Kent. So she had to go - trot on Sally.

Soon after Sally and I parted ways, our Sensei, Burt Meldon, a hairy welder with a strong Newcastle accent, was arrested and sentenced to seven years at her Majesty's Pleasure, for handling stolen goods. The club folded and Burt's membership of the national federation was also revoked, an aspect of the debacle I remember thinking of us unfairly severe. There was another karate club on the other side of town, but attending would have required father to forgo his glass of whiskey, get into a car and drive me across town. I knew this wasn't going to happen, so I feigned a loss of interest in karate, hung up my brown belt, and dedicated myself to improving my economic situation.

My entrepreneurial spirit drew me to a profitable but esoteric pursuit. The ancient tradition of wallfish wrangling. For those of you not in the know, wallfish is a colloquial English term for snails. I began by collecting slugs and snails from local gardens, for a small fee. Sometimes during the day but often at night with a torch, which was much more effective, for which I charged a slightly bigger fee. The snails I fattened up on fresh lettuce leaves in large plastic bins, before transferring them to clean plastic bins containing nothing but sand – after a week in those I sold the now 'flushed' snails to a local wannabe French bistro; I earned £20.00 every two weeks, doesn't sound much now but that was a lot of money back then. The slugs I executed on an anvil of death - the base of a birdbath that had been broken by our Jack Russell Wiggy - with a hoe. It was a very rewarding pursuit. The shudder of the hoe reverberating up my arm as it struck the stone, the crunch-splat as the gastropod burst, the smear that discoloured my anvil of death, it all enthralled me. Time well spent indeed, I mean, who needs boys when you have an anvil of death?

It may not surprise you to hear that my entrepreneurial zeal and my prudish outlook did nothing to enamour me to my peers, I was marked as "weird," I was called "frigid," I was deemed to be "stuck-up," and of course, as I had the face that could only be appreciated by a Pythagorean diagram, I must have been a lesbian. If making money from snails and not giving-out to the first lout in a football shirt who smiled at me made me "tight" – then I was as tight as a thumbscrew. If being frigid meant I wasn't turned on by the smell of Brut and unwashed armpits, then I was as frigid as a rock. If being stuck-up, meant I thought I was better than them, then yes guilty as charged, and as for being a lesbian… well I think it's too narrow a distinction. I think;

"that I possess a sense of naivety and open mindedness which enables me to see the world in a range of colours, not just the narrow spectrum, prescribed and sanctioned by society…"

No, I don't believe a word of it either but it's something I used to reel off to my prison therapist once a week, always worth a giggle. Anyhow, due to my perceived weirdo status, I never received any invitations to dances or teenage bottle spinning parties; also known as late-night date rape sessions – except for one, and I'll definitely get to that later, but the root of that debacle lays with "the regrettable incident."

The "regrettable incident," as Mr Ryley my school headmaster would later call it, occurred on a Thursday morning in my last year at school during a Physical Education lesson – if that's not an oxymoron I don't know what is. There was the usual blonde bottleneck as the netball divas rushed into the changing room, I waited for the nonsense to subside before I made my way in, hearing a noise behind me, and thinking it was our teacher Ms Biggadyke (not making that up), I caught the door and said, "there you go Miss." But it wasn't Ms Biggadyke, it was the head-girl and captain of the netball team, the gorgeous Brenda Parker – if cheerleaders had existed in England back then, she would have been that too. Chief Cheerleader, and wet-dream queen. Beautiful, curvy, straight-toothed, and full-breasted, a woman of experience at sixteen, basically a total slut. And she was gravely offended that I, an uptight, frigid, lesbo, weirdo, had confused her with Ms Biggadyke. She raised a perfectly manicured finger to my face, grabbed hold of my blouse and pushed me into the changing room, and proceed to give me a dressing down. I was liberally sprayed with the Bubblicious flavoured spital from her exquisitely lacquered lips. Two of her blonde handmaidens, Victoria Pris and Sophia Blume, swooped in behind me, and began to shove me around, as if I were one of their accursed netballs. I didn't put up much of a struggle until my backpack was wrenched from my hands and thrown across the changing room. It was a new bag and full of library books. I vividly remember Parker's mocking sneer; "what ya going to do about it freak." The room fell silent – a challenge had been made - and in that silence, I had a moment of clarity; I wasn't afraid, Parker was no threat to me, and I really wanted to do something about it. Parker lent in snarling, repeating the challenge; "what you going to do about it, you disgusting freak?"

I saw it play out in my head. My knee ramming into Parker's over exercised twat, a double Tsuki to her aerobicized gut, and my teeth sinking into her neck as she crumpled at my feet. Of course, I had to expect some resistance; the lacky bitches grabbing at my hair, trying to pull me off as the blood flowed, but a Ushiro Geri back kick, followed by a sweeping Masashi Geri roundhouse would have them sprawling. Then I'd grab their ponytails, pull them off balance and then ram their heads into the heavy black hooks fixed to the changing room walls. I'd finish, bloody and unbowed, stamping their faces into the floor. I could do it. I wanted to do it. But I also knew if I started, it would come true, I would not stop until my vision was fulfilled, I would kill them. It was a strange sensation. I felt sorry for them, and yet utterly deadly.

"What you going to do about it," Brenda sneered again– and something had to be done.

I grabbed hold of one of the black metal coat hooks, braced my leg against the wall and threw myself backwards. The dislocating pop echoed off the walls, causing three girls to vomit. I screamed, I'd never felt such pain and wanted the world to know it. Hearing the commotion, Ms Biggadyke (really not making that up) our hunchbacked P.E teacher (oxymoron) rushed in. Parker and her dolly dolts panicked, "it wasn't us, she did it to herself!" And who's going to believe that? No one, as it turned out.

"This is a regrettable incident," declared Mr Ryley the headmaster the next day in his office.

My father, in full wannabe lawyer mode – he was actually a minor clerk for a local legal firm - couldn't resist the opportunity to beat on an open door; "this would never have happened if the required adult supervision had been provided, this is a woeful and wanton act of neglect. Dereliction of duty is the root cause of this incident, and I want to know what you're going to do to ensure my daughter's safety when she's in your care." - my safety? what a wanker.

Parker was stripped of her netball captaincy, her position as head girl, and assigned litter duty for a month; alongside her two goony handmaidens. I was placed on protective detention for three months. All my lessons were to be taken in “Close Observation” – a tiny room usually frequented by students who enjoyed eating their own faeces. Every break and subsequent P.E lesson was to be spent in the school library. I played my part, by looking suitably crestfallen, but those were the best of my school days.

Suddenly I was the talk of the school, the nutjob that had slayed the dragon headed netball captain. I was a folk hero. Somehow, despite many witnesses, or perhaps because of them, the details of the “unfortunate event,” changed into something completely at odds with the truth, and I let them run with it. One consequence of my newfound notoriety was that I made a friend. Simon ‘Slightly’ Slater, was the tallest boy in our year, and he had been since the age of twelve. His aberrant physical peculiarity was enough to make Slater a target of bullying, but Slater had more to offer the thug mentality, he was a smorgasbord of bully appetisers, for Slater was undoubtably and undeniably gay. He ticked so many “nice boy” boxes, that if I were to list them here, you’d think him a attention seeking cliché, which he certainly wasn’t. The arbitrary fate of nature had merely pinned a double target to his back and placed him in a time called “WHEN FUCKING IDIOTS RULED THE EARTH!” (brought to you by selective narrow vision and mono sound) and that wasn’t Simon’s fault, he was just trying to be himself. We met in the library, during my mandated protective sentence.

I was sitting in a chair at the back of the room, reading about the seventeenth century's Witch Trials, when this long shadow fell over me and the scent of jasmine filled the air.

"I heard what you did in the gym," Slater beamed as he slumped down in the chair next to me, "girl you are the talk of the school."

"It was the changing room, not the gym."

"Whatever. I'm just so impressed," he produced a bag of crisps and began eating them – strictly forbidden in the library, "the arseholes had it coming. I wish I could have seen it. What did it feel like?"

"Feel like?"

"Yes, to beat them up. What did it feel like? Was it good?" I was offered a crisp, I declined on principle, "I heard you put two of them in hospital."

"No, I put myself in hospital. And it hurt. I dislocated my own shoulder, and they were suspended."

The crisp packet was thrust back into the coat pocket, "really?"

“Really. I staged the whole thing,” I had no idea why I was telling this wet boy the truth, but doing so felt right.

Slater’s eyes glowed, “oh my god! That’s amazing. My name’s Simon.”

“I know,” and I just had to ask, “why do they call you Slightly?”

Simon crossed his arms, and leant in, “it’s my bitch mother’s fault. Some arseholes on the PTA said I was feminine, the bitch answered, “only slightly.” Can you believe it? Next day its all-over school. Bitch. I’m not feminine. I just like boys.”

“Girls like boys. I think that’s what makes you feminine, liking boys.”

“Boys like girls, girls like boys, boys like boys, girls like girls. They can’t all be feminine. I’m not feminine, I’m gay.”

Such a statement may seem trivial now, totally unexceptional, but back then it took courage to say such things out loud. It was in fact the first time I had ever heard anybody claim the “gay” title for themselves. It was my turn to be impressed.

At that moment a passing cluster of junior no neck foreskins walked into the library, spotting us, one of them declared, “Look Slightly’s got a girlfriend!”

Simon recoiled from the blast of laughter, and dropped his head. I guess his courage only went so far, “sorry, I’ll let you get on.”

“Leave him alone,” I snapped.

“Oh yeah says who…” And then they saw who – the head girl slaying nutjob – the foreskins withered and retreated.

“That was amazing...” Slightly glowed and shuffled his chair forward, “what are you reading? Oh… witches. Somebodies got a kink!”

We were friends from that moment. But I have to confess, although I’ve often to risen to Simon’s defence, I only ever did it for my own pleasure. All in all, I did not treat Slater well. I’ll give you one example, but I assure you there were many. Soon after the above meeting, Slater and I were walking single file across the raised edge of the banked earthen sound barriers that run alongside the dual carriageways that split our council estate, Popley from the older Oakridge estate. It was a good spot to watch for traffic accidents. Slater was babbling on about Barbara Striesland or something or other, when I saw a flash of silver at my feet.

"A slowworm," I declared, bending down to pick it up. And in the amount of time it took to say those words, straighten my back, and hold out my hand – Slater was gone. He'd cleared a hundred yards in seconds.

"Put it down!" he screeched.

"It's only a slow worm," I protested, taking a step forward. Simon nearly bolted, so I put the back into the grass.

"Is it gone?"

"You saw me put it down. What was all that about?"

"Is it gone? I can't abide snakes."

"Abide? What are you, the archbishop of Canterbury? And anyway, it's not a snake, it's a…"

"I don't care. Put it down," Slater insisted, "put it down, just put it down!"

"I've put it down, it's gone. Calm down," I advanced hands raised in surrender, until I could place a hand on his arm, I'm barely five foot tall, so trying to reach his shoulder would have been ridiculous, "it wasn't a snake…"

"I don't care," Slater bristled.

"You will," I grabbed both is nipples and twisted. Slater fell to his knees and yelped like a puppy on a hotplate. "Don't interrupt me ever again. It wasn't a snake. I told you it wasn't a snake," I added another twist for emphasis, "I am the snake. I am the viper, and don't you ever raise your voice to me again," I snarled pushing him away, "I'm sick of men talking over me."

"You bitch, that hurt," Slater winced massaging his chest.

"You loved it."

"I did not!" he insisted.

"I beg to differ Slightly…" I pointed to his taut crotch, "in fact much more than slightly. Hello big boy."

Slater turned crimson, as he fought to push down his protruding pocket hump, "don't look, don't look!"

"It's okay, I don't mind," I stepped forward, slapped his face, grabbed his hair, and twisted his left nipple until he shivered, "there you go big boy, enjoy."

"You… biiiitch," Slater sighed with a shiver.

I stepped back and watched as a damp patch formed on the front of his grey stay-pressed slacks, "I need to go home and change," he mumbled shamefacedly, as he got to his feet and trotted off head bowed.

"Mind if I... come," I smirked.

No, I was not kind to Slater, but he never complained... again.

Slater had a huge boy crush on Jeremy Vincent, a boy that had been in the year above us and was now doing a Theatre Arts course at the local college. How to describe Jeremy? A hairdo with a vacant smile; a vacant smile with all the panache of a wet tissue; a wet tissue with a taste for cravats and an ego that could put Buckingham Palace in the shade – but Jeremy loved Jeremy. Tolerating Jeremy and still maintaining a functioning airway was just about all I could handle. Word reached Simon that Jeremy would be attending one of the college arty parties being held on the other side of the estate. Simon claimed that being openly gay entitled him to attend all arty house parties, and that I, by association would be welcome too. I guess, I was intrigued by the mystery and glamour of the fabled college crowd parties – it didn't last long. When we arrived at the same-as-same-as house, the place was already heaving, the air had been replaced by cigarette smoke, and the windows dripped with condensation. Just the right atmosphere for a budding yeast infection like Jeremy. As soon as we were through the door, Slater did this; "Jeremy, where's Jeremy? Has anybody seen Jeremy? Jeremy sweetie!" And disappeared off into the seething teenage Petri dish. Leaving me standing there, in full view of the gathered Brut boys, who were snorting like truffling hogs with the scent in their snouts. I backed away before they started drooling. I needn't have worried, nobody paid me the slightest bit of attention, my truffle was not in peril, and I didn't care. I was content to let the evening pass and look for amusing shapes in the whitewashed woodchip wallpaper. But the world would not let me be.

As some point I ventured back into the kitchen and grabbed a lukewarm beer, just as Paul Lawson walked through the door. Lawson was the square jawed, football captain heartthrob of the school, basically the least arty guy on the estate, but so 'cool' he also didn't need an invite. I'd never had any direct dealings with Lawson. I was well below the range of his testosterone fuelled radar - too ugly to consider, too sharp to taunt, and I'm sure I would have stayed that way if Brenda Parker, our recently disgraced netball captain, hadn't been Paul's bigtime squeeze. Netball captain and football captain – how predictable. So, you can understand why, when he swaggered into the room, I expected Brenda to totter in on his aftershave wake. But I was mistaken, she was not there, Paul was flying solo, and after grabbing a beer, he zoned in on me.

"Hi there, I'm Paul."

"I know who you are."

"Cool, I didn't know you'd be here."

"Why should you?"

"Don't be like that," he drawled with feigned injury, as if such a monumental ego could be pricked by such as I, "look whatever happened between you and B. it has nothing to do with me."

"Is Brenda coming?"

Paul gave me a leery wink, "don't worry she's still grounded. You're safe with me." Despite the rigid jawline, angular eyebrows and T-square shoulders, there was something oddly cephalopod about Lawson. Perhaps it was the way his eyes roamed over me, touching places he had no business even imagining, or the cold clammy hands that were brushing the hair away from my face, as they pulled me closer to his. When I resisted, he leaned in, mouth open, ready to tonsil gargle like some B-movie gigolo. I blocked him with a hand to his chest, but his weight pressed forward, pushing me backwards into the grating woodchip wall. As his lips zeroed in on mine, I clenched my teeth and squeezed my mouth tight. Our lips collided. He must have felt my resistance, it must have felt like kissing a fist, but he wasn't deterred, he just pressed in harder. His hand touched my throat, and squeezed, I opened my mouth to gasp, and he rammed his tongue into my mouth – I wish I'd bitten it off, but I didn't, I just froze, once again betrayed by my bodies inability to react. He stepped back and laughed in my face. I wanted to rip his throat out, but I stood there, frozen, stunned and fuming. I dropped the bottle of beer, a jet sprayed up from the bottle and doused his trousers, and the spell broke. I pushed past him, and marched out the front door, with Lawson's mocking laughter ringing in my ears. Fuck Lawson, fuck Slater, I was out of there.

2

It's widely known that the development of certain pathologies - that you may be considering I have - can be predicted by the subject's behaviour towards animals. And that is something I feel I need to address. It's true I had an animosity towards invertebrates, but nothing more than your average gardener is proud to profess. And I don't see why I should be judged for not killing as indiscriminately as many gardens do - I didn't litter gardens with slug traps or poisonous pellets that could have harmed other animals. I merely dispatched my harvest of Phylum Mollusca, with a hoe. And yes, it is true, I did once endanger the lives of twelve guineapigs in one night, but that was an act of retribution, and I got no pleasure from it. But I'll get to that later. My point is I have never gained pleasure from inflicting pain of animals. Quite the opposite, as the ledger entry a week before my sixteenth birthday clearly illustrates; "lost Wiggy, feel shitty."

I was making myself a cup of tea standing by the kitchen sink, and quite by accident overpoured the mug. The spillage flowed from the countertop, and onto the back of our Jack Russel terrier Wiggy, causing him to run about the kitchen in a howling panic. I did not enjoy it. I had grown up with that dog and had never before caused him any pain or discomfort in any way shape or form; I happen to think the dumb beast actually liked me. I was appalled by what had happened. I saw his distress and felt it. I felt remorse even though it had been a genuine accident – it was an appalling experience, overwhelming and unbearable. I felt as if my heart was about to explode. And I knew, I swore, I could never allow myself to feel such an intensity of emotion ever again, it had to be controlled. But how? I could see no other way of doing it but by taming the emotion. And how does one tame any emotion? By exposure to it of course. So, I dropped some more hot water on Wiggy's back, and then some more, until the feeling was burnt, or should I say, scalded away. And when we buried Wiggy that night, I believe we buried my ability to empathise with humanity alongside him, and his squeaky toy. I promise you I was heartbroken and hollow. The void has remained with me ever since. And why would I want to fill it? How does it benefit a person to feel others pain, in a world filled with pain? And while we're about it, let's talk about remorse. Remorse is a retrospective concept. You can feel happy or glad, before or after an event. You can even feel guilty before taking action; feeling guilt for thinking is not unusual, but remorse is defined by action? You only get remorse once you've acted and seen the consequences of those actions. And even then, you're relying on the much-vaunted capacity of empathy, which being a woman, I am instinctively meant to have an abundance of… answer me this; have you ever been with a bunch of girls talking about period pain? Let me tell you this, empathy runs dry pretty-damn quick. Remorse is a mugs game, and I'm no mug, I'm the sneaky viper, so watch out world – keep back.

"Do you want to stay over?" Slater asked as he danced about his bedroom. He had a habit of inflicting his latest musical infatuations, and their accompanying dance moves upon me – if Duran Duran saw what he did with Wild Boys they'd weep for shame.

"No, I do not."

"Why? You know you're perfectly safe with me. I've stayed at yours, but you never stay here, how come?"

"I dream."

"Oh, we all do that," he sniggered and then stopped dancing and frowned, "…do girls do that too? Or do you mean you wet the bed?"

"No, I mean I dream. I have nightmares, and sometimes I sleepwalk."

"Really? Is it juicy? Do tell, I have this recurring dream where I'm locked in this sauna with the entire male cast of Grange Hill, it's very exciting."

"Sounds delightful, you twisted beanpole. I dream about a giant blood red rhinoceros."

Slater supressed a laugh, I didn't supress my glare, he rallied with a flick of his too blonde locks, "oh come on, that doesn't sound too bad. What does it do? Serenade you with Disney hits from beneath your window?"

"Do? It doesn't do anything. It stands under my window, breathing?"

"Is that it? It breathes," his plucked eyebrows narrowed, "I wonder what it wants? What does it want?"

"How should I know? It's a giant blood red rhino, what do you think it wants?"

"I don't know, it's your dream. But when I was little, I use to have nightmares and my mother, the bitch, told me to ask them what they wanted, so I did, and they stopped. You should ask your rhino what it wants?"

"I don't talk rhinoceros."

"It's a Disney dream. Talking animals. Perhaps it wants to show you something? It might be lucky; you should follow it and see what happens."

"Follow it? Have you ever had a falling dream? Apparently, if you don't wake up before you hit the ground you die. What do you think will happen if I get stomped by a giant lucky rhino in my dream?"

"Firstly, that's nonsense," Slater gyrated his hips as he placed his hands on his chest protecting his nipples, "that's the kind of crap they put in Cosmo just to fill up space. And frankly, I'm surprised you didn't know that," I attempted to pinch his thigh, but he sidestepped me with a shimmy and a perfectly executed heel to heel slide, "stop it! Listen, you should definitely follow your rhino, talk to it … befriend it. Give it an apple and see what happens!"

"Give it an apple?"

"A nice crisp Granny Smith, they're rhinos' favourites, everybody knows that darling."

"Everybody?"

"Everybody and his sodding wife," and we both laughed until our sides hurt.

Slater could do that, make me laugh, that's probably why I let him live.

As I mentioned, my sixteenth year was not a great year for me, there was not a lot to laugh about; my dog died, and my father remarried. Her name was Gladys, she was ten years younger than my father, and worked as some kind of secretary or clerk at his office. She was bright-eyed, tall, and slim but with a shapely frontage. I'm sure many considered her a fine catch. I saw many men give my father a sly wink and a thumbs up when we all went out together. I however, saw her more of a snag than a catch, a snag that had to be dealt with before the whole garment of my life was unravelled. On reflection, this was nothing more than a case of infantile insecurity, the raging jealousy of a humdrum Electra complex - that I had neither the wit nor capacity to manage. But how can I apologise for not being emotionally developed at the age of sixteen? And what good would it do? Afterall, Gladys is no-longer with us.

Gladys was generous with her time, money and her affection; I cannot fault her for trying. Perhaps if she hadn't been involved with my father and I hadn't been a selfish brat I may have been able to bear her vacuous presence, but I wasn't, and I couldn't, I simply loathed her. Her pretty smile made me tense, her sing-song voice made me retch, and her sickly-sweet scent made my head spin. I was in a perpetual state of seasickness whenever I was in her presence. I could see she was making my father happy, as I said he actually stopped drinking, and something about that was just unseemly. It boiled my piss, that he wasn't willing to stop drinking for me – but for Miss Have Tits Will Travel, anything was possible. Even my ability to unnerve him was quelled by Gladys' presence. And yet, when he asked me if I minded if they married, I said no.

The wedding was a small registry office affair, dull but blessedly brief, which is just as well, because Gladys put me in a pink dress with white trimming…think about that, pink with white trim - I looked like a set of Laura Ashley curtains. Pink and white, cute and sweet – they were damned lucky the service was short… people would have died. Afterwards we went out for a meal at the wannabe French bistro that bought my snails, and I got changed in the toilets. They had the smallest toilet cubicle I had ever encountered; I scrapped both my elbows getting changed in that damn thing; I also remember ordering a very un-French burger as an act of revenge, and it was then that Gladys questioned my order; "does the bun have sesame seeds? Sorry to have to ask but I'm horribly allergic to sesame seeds."

"Really? I didn't know that," father responded, "how allergic?"

"Horribly," she informed us.

I instantly logged this information and locked it away for further consideration. I gave Gladys six months to stop being so "very Gladys;" I marked the date in my ledger alongside the escalating slug deaths and waited. But the woman couldn't help herself. She offered to help me with my homework, came to my school open evening, and treated Slater with kindness and respect every time he came round - which was far too often - feeding him with toast and jam and listening to his banal Barbara Streisand obsession. They even sang together. But she finally crossed the line three days before her six-month probation period had ended. She bought me a fantastically illustrated edition of "Der Hexenhammer; Malleus Maleficarum," – the Hammer of the Witches. I was furious. Why? Because she saw me, because she was encroaching into my territory! My fascinations were my business. I didn't want them sullied by her Gladysness. I didn't sleep well that night. And then sometime around two in the morning, I heard a deep, snuffling rumble beneath my window. Even before I looked, I knew the beast was back. I looked out my window and there it was, glinting like a scarlet flame in the streetlights, so huge I could have reached out of my window and touched the tip of its single horn. I told myself I was tired, I told myself I was dreaming, even though I could feel the cold night air against my skin, but as it had to be a dream I decided to follow Slightly's guidance and get into the dream. I grabbed my dressing gown, went downstairs and out the front door to confront the beast. I forgot the apple.

As long and as broad as a bus, it stood at the end of our path. Its breath was hot and moist and clung to my skin like a wet flannel. It saw me and lowered its head in recognition, its fist-sized eyes glowing like blood red moons. I saw my reflection in their bloom, and knew, knew for certain, that it knew me. Slowly it turned away, walking with slow ponderous footsteps I could feel reverberating in my teeth. I stood there, the cold night air eating through my dressing gown, watching it go. I caught myself thinking; if this is a dream, I really should wake up and pull my bed covers back on, before I get cold and wake myself up, or I'll never find out where this thing is going. And then I was chasing after it.

The beast lumbered slowly along the estates access road and then turned towards the underpass that joined our estate to Oakridge. It lowered its head, twisting its horn to one side as it stepped into the tunnel – "You'll get stuck," I heard myself say, and then it was gone. And there I was, cold, awake and alone standing before a darkened underpass that stank of stale vomit and piss; dressed in a nightie and a flimsy dressing gown, wondering what the hell had just happened. Confounded and confused I hurried back home, keeping to the shadows, ears alert to every sound, watching for the perverts that lurked in every doorway; until breathless and frozen, I reached our doorstep. I didn't have a key so had to ring the doorbell. Gladys answered the door dressed in a glowing silk nightdress that made her look like a sexy Christmas angel.

"Oh my… what are you doing out of bed? How did you get out here?" It was a reasonable question given the circumstances.

"I think I sleepwalked again," I replied, a reasonable reply given the options I had.

"Oh, you poor love, come in, come in, you must be frozen, I'll make you a hot chocolate and you can tell me all about it."

"There's nothing to tell. I sleepwalk… sometimes… I have nightmares."

"Did you have a nightmare tonight? What if something had happened to you? Does your father know you do this?"

"Of course he knows. Did I have a nightmare? Well, a blood red rhinoceros woke me up, so I followed it through the estate, does that sound like a nightmare to you?"

Gladys' face jerked from alarm to consternation, I could tell she was trying to process my information, "has this happened before? Does it happen, say the week or so before your period? I've read somewhere that can happen. Perhaps we should see a doctor, talk to him about, contraception, just to regulate your menstrual cycle, it might help?"

It was decided; I had to kill Gladys.

Although it pained me to alter my plans, ruin my ledger and cut short my six-month deadline, I figured the outcome was bound to be the same. Gladys wasn't going to modify her ways in three days, so I had to bear the discomfort or changing my plans and be flexible. It was an important life lesson.

Three days later, I was ready to build on my Raymond Ekal experience and apply my learning. I was having breakfast alone in the kitchen, when I heard Gladys's scream, followed by a crash, a gasp of horror and a moment of exquisitely tense silence, shattered by a heavy thud and my fathers' anguished cries. Father nearly fell down the stairs to get the living room phone – imagine that kids, a static phone you have to walk towards to use! Panicked and spluttering, father tried to call for an ambulance, by screaming down the wrong end of the phone, not a great technique. During the commotion, I sneaked upstairs, peaked into the bathroom, and there was Gladys's frothing like a first-year science experiment volcano – nothing doing there – so into the bedroom I went, ticking off my list as I went;

A) Find the Sesame Snap smeared lipstick – check.

B) Replace Sesame Snap smeared lipstick with another of an identical make and shade which Gladys had "misplaced" two months previously…

- check.

C) Dispose of Sesame Snap – as good as – ate it and stuffed wrapper down knickers for later disposal.

N.B – Sesame Snaps are a safe and delightful snack you can buy from any health food shop at an amazingly cheap price.

The irony of my first victim being my mother or at least a mother, is not wasted on me. If my mother had succeeded in killing me, then my mother may have lived, but my other mother certainly wouldn't have died. That night, as father howled and drank, I took a walk down to the underpass to see if the night rhino would come to reward or punish me for my actions – he did not show. I told myself it had better places to be, but I had to wonder, had my actions been promoted by a nightmare or a vision; and then I threw the lipstick and the Sesame Seed wrapper into a bush.

The accepted wisdom would have us believe that serial killers have a type, a taste if you will, that they will not stray from - such twisted souls belong to a psychopathy that I - as I'm sure you can tell - am trying to distance myself from, I am not one of their number, I am something far worse. I killed another woman, a completely unsisterly, non-feminist move, and she would not be my last, but I assure you my female victims would be greatly outweighed by the many, many men to fall under my hand. So, I don't have a type, I'm an equal opportunity killer – male, female, old or young, I'm really not fussed. Therefore, not a serial killer something far, far worse.

So, let's get to the guineapigs. I just know you're dying to hear all about it. Now I have to say although I do pride myself in having an excellent memory for details and dates, but on checking my ledger, it seems I was a few months out, as I thought this took place a few weeks after Gladys' demise but in fact it was a full three months later, at Christmas, three months before my seventieth birthday. All I can think is that Christmas that year must have been a dull affair because I've no recollection of it at all. I guess father had other things on his mind. So let me set the scene; we lived in a small, terraced house, third from the end; just another same-as-same-as house – seven doors down from an elderly gentleman called Mr Pole.

Mr Pole was one of those men that parents used to tell their children to avoid; "if Mr Pole offers you sweets don't take them," or "if Mr Pole says would you like to see his guineapigs, say no." Why this was so, was never expanded upon, you were just expected to take it on trust that your parents knew what they were talking about – I found this a challenge. My imagination used to run wild, was Mr Pole like the witch from Hansel and Gretal, or the troll from the Three Billy Goats Gruff? Why was this grey unassuming man so dangerous? And what was this thing about guineapigs? Even when they showed us a "Stranger Danger," film in primary school I didn't make the connection, although that may have been due to the actor in the grainy projected film baring an uncanny resemblance to my father rather than the sheeplike Mr Pole. So, I always made a point of saying hello to Mr Pole, and he would always raise his hand and garble an unintelligible greeting in return. I never had any problems with Mr Pole, perhaps I wasn't his type.

It was a Saturday, and I was walking into town when I saw a small crowd gathered around a bus stop. There were three mothers with small children and an elderly woman, and a certain mouth-breather called Boosey, a broad chested oaf with a shaved head and the prerequisite bother-boy oxblood bother-boots. Something or someone was writhing on the floor before them. I hurried over to find Mr Pole locked into a thrashing fit. Bloodied foam was pouring from his mouth, a dark stain spreading from the centre of his worn grey slacks. One of the mother's stepped forward to assist him, but Boosey grabbed her by the arm and said, "leave him be, he's a nonce." The woman, Boosey's wife as it turned out, tried to pull herself clear of his grip but Boosey held fast. The children were crying, their mother was cursing but Boosey insisted, "I said leave him be, he's a fucking nonce." And then the bus arrived, Boosey stepped over Mr Pole, taking his wife with him, and bawling at the three children to follow. It was then that the bus driver saw the commotion and grabbed his cab handset. He left the bus to assist Mr Pole. I must say that I was so moved by his actions that for years later I considered bus driver to a be noble profession. I even considered joining their ranks. I think we can all agree that it's been to everybody's benefit that I didn't answer that calling - how easy the slaughter would have been, a bus at a time, but I digress. The ambulance arrived some ten minutes later, and poor Mr Pole was carted off still quivering like a startled dog. Two days later I overheard a neighbour, Janice from next door, informing my father that Mr Pole had died, an epileptic seizure that refused to stop, until it stopped his heart.

"Is it true he kept guineapigs? I blurted, "are they okay?"

"Don't worry about them sweetie, Mr Pole took good care of them, they'll have water for days yet," Janice twittered in a condescending manner that set my teeth on edge.

"But what if they haven't?" I protested with more of a growl than I intended.

"I think Edna has a key, she cleans for him twice a week," Janice replied, pointing to the house directly opposite ours, as she directed her answer towards my father.

"We'd better check," my father sighed despondently.

"I'll do it," I volunteered, my father didn't have the energy to refuse.

Edna, the heroic dinner lady, was called upon, and the three us; twittering Janice, Edna and I marched over to Mr Pole's house.

The smell of tainted wet straw hit me as soon as I stepped through the door, followed quickly by the buzzing of flies.

"Oh dear, I think he's late changing their straw again," Edna huffed and then, possibly realising the past tense would have been more appropriate, added, "bless him."

The front room was crammed full of large cages, three ran across the wall under the window, with more, stacked three high against the opposite wall. This left a narrow passage between the door we'd come through and the door to the adjoining room. The cages were still, silent and seemingly empty.

"Are they dead?" Janice whispered swiping at a fly.

"No Janice, they're asleep," Edna replied with a snort, "tucked away in their little beds sleeping like the …" she didn't complete the sentence but checked her rollers, swiped at a fly and then continued in a lowered voice. "They mostly come out at night. God knows what will happened to the little buggers now."

"How many are there?" I asked.

"I haven't a clue, thirty maybe more," saying this Edna bumped the side of the nearest cage with her prodigious hip, eliciting a chorus of high-pitched squeaks and a fresh wave of irritated flies, "there you go, they're alive. I don't know what he saw in them, I surely don't."

"Didn't he have any family the poor thing?" Janice whined – honestly the more I recall of this woman the more baffled I am that I let her live.

"Him, nah. All killed in the war. Let's get away from these damned flies. Come look here, you'll like this young'un," Edna led the way through the passage of cages and took us into the kitchen. The two rooms couldn't have been more different. Whereas the previous room had been thick with feted air, buzzing flies and the stink of incarcerated animals, the kitchen was pristine, shinning white, and the walls were smothered with perfectly aligned framed photographs, paintings, and prints, all with one theme, R.A.F bombers.

"Look here," Edna pointed to a large framed black and white photo of a young, uniformed airman and a set of six ribboned medals.

"That's never him," Janice gasped.

"It is. A hero he was. A proper bloody hero. Twenty-five raids. Shot down over France, captured, the whole bit. That's when he got his head injury, it was so bad the Germans sent him back. Oh, I know what people said about him. People can be cruel. If there were any justice in this world, there's some that should be ashamed. Bloody hero he was, poor old bugger."

"To die like that, such a shame, such a shame," Janice observed – what a wet fart of a woman.

"As I hear it the bastards stepped over him."

"No, they never did."

"That's what I hear."

I looked into the eyes of the young man in the photo, playful eyes full of hope. Yes, step over him they did, and called him names as he lay twitching in his own piss.

Bastards they were indeed. I can't say why I was so moved, but I knew right there and then, there had to be a reckoning.

I knew where Boosey lived because everybody knew where Boosey lived. It was 'that house' on the estate, every estate has one. It was three blocks back from my own terrace, but the dull thud of pounding music would often reach us, that or screamed obscenities or terrified screams. It was the house to hurry past. But all that weekend, I watched that house from a distance, I saw Boosey come and go, discarding fag ends and beer bottles left, right and centre, and contemplated how to exact justice. I hate litter bugs.

That Monday, straight after school I called on Edna and asked her if she had any news on the fate of the guineapigs. She told me; "I called the RSPCA. But they haven't got back to me yet. But they'd better get a move on as the council will be here in a day or two to clear the house."

"What will happen to his medals?"

"They'll sell 'em off or dump 'em. Why? Do you want them? Better you have them than one of those sticky-fingered council workers. Go on, you go get them," and she handed me the key.

An unexpected reward, I'd planned to use the guineapigs as an excuse to gain access, but this was even better, "I'll check on the guineapigs when I'm there."

"Take a couple of them home with you too if you like, God knows there's enough of the buggers to go around. Make sure you lock up you hear? And bring the key back."

I heard. I let myself in, marched into the kitchen, removed Mr Poles framed photo with the medals from the wall, put it under my arm, and proceeded to unlock the backdoor, with the key that was hung beside it. Edna was waiting by her open door when I emerged, her hand beckoning for the key.

"Good girl. You got it then? Now you look after that."

"I will, I'm going to research it, do a project, find out all about him, I might even write a piece for the local paper."

"You do that, I might even read it. Right then, off you trot."

And trot I did.

That night I slung my backpack over my shoulder and snuck out through the back garden into the alley beyond – leaving unnoticed wasn't exactly a challenge once father had demolished a bottle of whiskey. I counted the back gates and slipped over the fence into Mr Poles back yard. Torch in hand I tested the backdoor, it opened soundlessly. I removed an empty beer bottle the two fag ends I'd collected from outside Boosey's place from my backpack, and then quickly filled it with twelve squeaking guineapigs. I then locked the door behind me and exited the garden with the key in my back pocket. The next phase was not going to be so easy, or as pleasant.

Firstly, I had to wait, crouching in a stinking back alley, with a backpack full of squeaking rodents, a nerve-racking experience I can assure you. And secondly, I had to endure the torrent of bile and abuse flooding from that house. The kids would scream and Boosey would yell, then Boosey yelled, and the kids screamed, or Boosey yelled at his wife, so she screeched at him, and then the kids would scream, and then Boosey would yell and she'd scream and the kids would scream; how his neighbours refrained from killing the lot of them is beyond me. Eventually the crying and yelling dissipated; the blaring TV went off and the lights upstairs went out. I threw the guineapigs - under arm - over the fence into the backyard, followed by Mr Poles backdoor key.

Three days later I was visited by one D.S Sims, a tall man with an unfortunate ginger tinge to his greying hair. We spoke in our kitchen, in front of my sozzled father – enjoying his role as "responsible adult," no matter how inappropriate the title was at that juncture.

"I've been speaking to your neighbour, Edna…"

"I advise you to say nothing, you're not obliged to say anything," father slurred.

"I haven't asked anything yet Mr Thornberry… the thing is, your neighbour, Edna said she gave you the key to the house, to check on Mr Pole's guineapigs." No mention of her gifting the picture? Edna was clearly covering my arse, as well as her own; unless of course, I was being played. "Did you for any reason go into the kitchen?"

"Yes, I went into the kitchen."

"Why? The guineapigs were in the front room."

"I went into the kitchen to get Mr Pole's medals. Edna said I could have them, otherwise the sticky-fingered council workers would sell them for beer."

D.S Sims smiled, I figured I'd just passed some kind of truth test, "did you happen to see the backdoor key when you were in there?"

"No, I don't think so."

"Do you know where the key was kept?"

"No."

"Did you unlock the backdoor?"

"No, I didn't have the key."

"But the door was locked. Did you test the back door to see if it was locked?"

"No."

"Not at all?"

"No, why would I?"

The problem was, I'd over planned my crime and thought too little about it from the vantage point of the objective observer. I'd given the police a plethora of evidence, too much evidence. There were the guineapigs at Boosey's house, as well as the beer bottle and fag-ends found at Mr Pole's house – all fine and dandy, but the backdoor key was a step too far. Why had the house raider locked the door behind him? Why were the keys found in Boosey's garden and not in his house, but more importantly, as there was no evidence of a break-in, how had Boosey acquired the key? It looked like a stitch-up and although the police were more than happy to accept the evidence against Boosey as genuine, Boosey's barristers weren't. He got off scot-free. Thankfully, the general public are much more gullible and not so forgiving. The entire family were hounded off the estate within six months. His wife eventually dealt with Boosey herself – as I heard it, he died from septicaemia, after she nailed his scrotum to a bedpost with a rusty nail – she got away with it by stating it was part of their regular "love play." Each to their own, who am I to judge? Personally, I like to think she reclaimed her agency, via a rusty nail. And the lesson we should take from this? Keep things simple, don't be clever, be simple - and I think this is a great life lesson for us all – at the end of the day, if you want someone dead, keep it simple and get the job done.

Six months later, June 6th to be exact, I returned home to find the coroners' report on Gladys' death had finally been delivered to our house. The verdict was accidental death. Cause of death, anaphylactic shock, probably due to the overly sedentary use of a tampon. It seemed my timing was better than I knew; had I waited another three days, an acceptable alibi would not have been in situ.

Father, who was already over self-medicating, didn't take the news well and began to self-medicate by the tumbler full. Why he should take the news so poorly perplexed me, what did he expect the report to say? That Gladys was less dead? I on the other hand was bursting with an exuberance I could barely contain; I may even have been humming! Father shot me a warning look; "what are you so happy about?"

"I'm not, perhaps I'm relieved. You hear about all these tests they can do, so you can never be too sure…"

"What are you talking about? What tests? What are you talking about?"

"You know tests, to determine cause of death. I'm just relieved its over that's all, it's over. We can move on."

"Move on? Move on! You never liked Gladys; you never even gave her a chance. Don't deny it, you're glad she's…" he spluttered to a halt, downed a glass, coughed and ploughed on, "if someone told me you'd … I wouldn't be at all surprised …" his face suddenly turned a sickly green, and he vomited all over himself.

"Careful father, imagine if that had happened in your sleep, with no-one around to save you," I chided, "I mean, one death in the house I can get away with but two?" I heard the words as they left my mouth – as did my father, I saw a connection spark behind his eyes,

"What did you do…" he rose from his seat, rocked on his heels, and fell forwards, crashing through the glass top of the coffee table. I looked for signs of blood, saw none, and considered utilizing a shard of glass – and then father snorted, farted and rolled onto his side.

I stood there shaking. Had I confessed? If not, it was pretty damn close. Would father remember? Why had I been so stupid, so boastful? They say every murderer wants to be caught – I'd never believed it, but there was no hiding from the evidence – evidently I couldn't keep my trap shut, did that mean I wanted to be caught? I grabbed my coat and announced to no one; "I'm going to see Slater. You… sleep it off." I sprinted into the underpass, driven to earth, seeking shelter from the storm in the stink of piss.

Successive waves of louts had ripped or blown out the underpass's lights so many times the council refused to replace them more than once a year. But I didn't mind the gloomy half-light or the reek of piss – it all seemed horribly appropriate that night.

I leant against the wall, comforted by the rough Artexed texture I could feel pressing into my back; and waited for my heart to stop dancing a jig. I tried talking myself into thinking that the chances of father remembering a word I'd said were virtually nil. But I wasn't easily convinced. Perhaps all I had to do was pretend nothing had happened. go home, act surprised when I saw the smashed coffee table and carry-on as before… and if he did remember, then I'd have to make sure he died of an accidental head injury, all the evidence was already there waiting for me to use it… it might even be easier just to go with that plan. All I had to do was get home before he woke up and finish the job, but I had been right.... two bodies in such quick succession would look very suspicious. I headed further into the tunnel, I needed to think. I was about six yards in when the tornado hit. And when I say tornado, that's exactly what I mean – the air was sucked to the far end of the tunnel dragging, leaves and litter past me at sped. As I watched the air seemed to thicken as the debris coalesced into a spinning funnel that began ricocheting from wall to wall as it howled down the tunnel towards it. It hit me with a full body blow that knocked the air out of me, lifted me off my feet and smashed me into the tunnels roof with such force I saw a spiral galaxy of stars. I was thrown out of the spiral, dazed, dizzy and bruised from arse to elbow. And then, silence, the wind was gone. A took a deep breath and instantly heard a scream and jeering coming from the other end of the underpass. Three figures, silhouetted in the light were gathered around a fourth, and they were intent on giving that person a hard time. I had my own problems, my head was spinning and everything ached like buggery, so I turned my back on them, and made my way back out of the tunnel - and then I heard a woman scream followed by a peel of mocking laughter; I spun myself around and marched down the tunnel, my rage ignited; “you there! Stop that at once!”

“Look what we got here,” a pig-faced lout with greasy shoulder length hair snorted, “you want some too. The more the merrier that’s what …” whatever the pig was going to snort next was left unsnorted, as my fist splattered his ugly snout. He staggered backwards, legs wobbling and began a slow, scraping descent down the artexed wall. Startled the other two louts, stood there bouncing on their toes, like bad Bruce Lee impersonators, not knowing what to do next; “Run!” I roared at them, “Run!” and they did, at least to the mouth of the underpass. I turned my attentions back to my bloodied foe, who was now on his knees, and landed a swift punch to his left ear.

“Leave him alone bitch!” one of his boys yelled, taking a step forward.

“Make me,” I grinned, “after all, I’m only a girl,” I took hold of the bleeders ear and dragged him to the tunnels entrance. The taller of his two comrades found some courage and took a step forward fists raised - so I stuck my thumb in his friend’s eye, “I wouldn’t, not unless you want him to lose an eye.”

“Bitch! Leave him alone.”

“Again with the bitch, that’ll cost you…” I pressed my thumb home. The pig thrashed, broke free of my grip and rolled away, to lay quaking at their feet.

“There you go, he’s all yours.”

“Bloody dyke lesbian! We’ll get you for this,” the smaller of the two snarled.

“I’m right here.” I spat back, taking a step forward, “why wait?” They picked up their buddy and fled.

As I turned back to the shadows, a girl stepped towards me, pulling her blouse tight around her chest – and I saw, in the same instant that she saw, that she was me.

Startled she stepped out of the underpass and into the orange glow of the streetlight and vanished – as in disappeared – as in gone, and a moment later, I heard “god good, what the hell was that!” echo down from the other end of the underpass; followed by the pounding of frantic steps as she – that is I- came running towards me, arms waving, wailing like a child after a nasty fall. It was frankly embarrassing to see, myself behaving so. I stepped back, letting her pass by, watched her exit the tunnel, and disappear. She reappeared again at the Popley end of the tunnel, “what’s happening?” she yelled.

"I have no idea!" I yelled back.

"I'm losing my mind!" again she ran forwards, hands buried in her hair, like a frantic victim from some disaster movie, but this time I stepped toward her and she came to a whirling halt six yards from me.

"Stop. Just calm down… are you hurt? Did they hurt you, are you okay?"

"Of course I'm not okay you're a doppelgänger," she said projecting an accusatory finger in my direction.

"I'm not a doppelgänger, you're the doppelgänger," I snapped back.

"No I'm not. I know who I am. You're the doppelgänger, you're the doppelgänger not me!"

"I am not!" I insisted, stepping forward.

"Stay where you are!"

"I'm not going to hurt you."

"Of course, you're going to hurt me you're a doppelgänger, that's what doppelgängers do."

“I just rescued you, remember that. You should be thanking me. Who were those creeps, I didn’t recognise them.”

“Just creeps from my school, they followed me from town. I shouldn’t have used the underpass…”

“Fuck that, it wasn’t your fault. You can walk anywhere you damn well like. Creeps like that need to be taught a lesson, and they got one tonight.”

“That’s true… it was impressive. I could never do that. And that just proves you’re the doppelgänger, not me.”

“If that’s the case. I would have let them rape you. Kill you and dump your body up there of the dual carriage way. But I didn’t did I? I saved you. Is that what doppelgängers do?”

She stood before me, just out of touching distance, crossed her arms and scowled; I had no idea I looked so fierce, like a witch about to throw a child into an oven, “what’s happening?”

“I haven’t a clue, but… stop scowling at me, this is not my fault, and you look like one of the Weird Sisters, stop it.”

She held her ripped blouse tight across her chest, and flattened her tousled hair, “I’m frightened that’s all.”

I looked her up and down; and I have to say, it was an uncanny experience to actually be beside myself, and apart from her horrendously sensible square toed Clarkes, we were identically dressed, "you know, you look pretty good. I'm surprised."

"I know… I thought I was fatter. I like your baseball boots."

She was lying – she said it with a fixed grin - but I let it go, "thanks, pleased to meet you," I held out my hand with my best grin stuck to my face.

"Better not, the world might explode or something."

"And we wouldn't want that would we..."

"Definitely not."

"What do you say to the idea that we both try stepping out of this end of the tunnel; together at the same time, and see what happens…" I suggested.

"What do you think will happen?"

"I don't know, end of the world maybe?"

"That's not funny," she snapped, "this is really weird, you do know how weird this is right? Why is this happening?

We shouldn't be doing this, you shouldn't be here, I'm not doing this."

"Oh for God's sake get a grip. It doesn't matter how many times you say it shouldn't be happening, it is happening, so deal with it."

"I'm scared."

"Well don't be, it's annoying…come on, together now."

We stood side-by-side, walked to the edge of the tunnel, and stepped beyond it, and she was gone. I turned around and there she was at the other end of the underpass.

"I don't like this!" she shouted, sounding like the petulant teenager I knew I was, "I don't understand! Why are you still there and I'm here, what does it mean?"

"Do I like a scientist to you? Look in the mirror, you're not."

"And you're not very nice. You're an evil doppelgänger and… and…I'm going home."

"No wait! You can't go…"

"You can't tell me what to do! I'm going home," She stepped out of the underpass, and disappeared like a whiff of smoke wafted through a beam of light. I stood there waiting for her to reappear... I waited twenty minutes and then I had to accept she/ I was gone.

Nonplussed, pissed and aching from head to toe, I made my way home. I stood on my doorstep, put the key in the door, but it didn't fit. I rang the bell, and when it chimed, I didn't recognise the chime, and when it opened, I realised the door had changed colour – and there was Slater standing holding the door open, "hay, alright? Come in."

"What are you doing here?"

"What d'you mean? I'm waiting for you Einstein, come on in, I've got everything set up."

As I stepped inside, Slater leant forward and kissed me, kissed me on the lips; "what the hell do you think you're playing at?"

"Nothing…are you okay?"

"What do you mean, nothing…" And then I saw the décor, the wallpaper, everything was wrong. It wasn't my house. It was Slater's house, "what's going on here?" And then I really did fall on my face.

"Oh my God, are you okay? Did you hurt yourself?" Slater rattled as he stood there doing nothing.

"What's happening?"

Slater looked baffled, "you fell over. Did you bang your head?"

"I'm fine, stop fussing," I slapped away Slater's offered hand and got myself off the floor, "I mean, what's happening here… now."

"History revision remember, are you alright?"

"I'm fine, don't ask again," I made my way into the kitchen, and found myself in a dining room, that should have been a kitchenette. The wall that shouldn't have been there was covered with photos of baby Slater and his proud grinning parents. I slumped down in a chair and buried my spinning head in a pile of textbooks and notepads.

"You should probably eat something, luckily I have something prepared," Slater disappeared into the kitchen, returning moments later carrying a plate of Mr Kipling's fondant fancies. "Want one? Help yourself. I think we should start with the stuff we did this year, because its fresher in our minds and then work our way backwards to the first year, agreed?" Slater nattered on, a black Bic pen behind his ear like he was some kind of hip woodwork teacher. This was not my hapless, arty Slater, this was a different Slater – and I didn't like it.

“My head hurts, I think I’m going crazy.”

“You did hit your head! We should go to A&E?”

“I said I’m fine don’t fuss. I just need to think, give me some air,” I pushed him aside and marched into the kitchen through the backdoor and into the garden – but not my garden, a horrific parody of a Japanese Zen Garden that could only have been created by a devotee of the T.V series Monkey. I could feel my stomach turning over as the grinning concrete Buddhas phased in and out of focus.

“Do want a drink of water?” Slightly asked as he rushed to my side.

I shut my eyes and tried to focus, “When did we first meet?”

“How do you mean?”

“I mean exactly what I said, do you remember how we first met?” I snapped.

“Ballroom dancing class, if you can’t remember that we really need to get you to A&E.”

The Buddhas were grinning at me, and I didn’t like it. I stormed back into the house, went straight to the pile of textbooks, picked one at random, and flicked through it –

everything seemed the same, 1066 blah-blah-blah, Corn Laws blah-blah-blah, Victorian England and the Industrial Revolution blah-blah-blah, World War II blah-bloody-blah. Everything was as it should be, even Florence Nightingale was still an outrageous bore; and yet somehow it all felt wrong. I knew this was not my world, just as this house was no longer my home.

"Know anything about alternate worlds?" I asked.

"What? Like Mars?"

"No, not Mars…don't be dense, alternate timelines, dimensions that kind of thing..."

"Like Alice in Wonderland? Have you been chasing rabbits?"

"Do be quiet, let me think…"

And what did I know about alternate realities? Sod all; just TV, comic book stuff and that's nothing to base a plan of survival on. Did I consider the dangers and complexity of transversing interdimensional time-space anomalies, the inherent danger of interacting with a timeline in which I was basically someone else? No, of course not. I thought about all the possibilities to be had in a doppelgänger world; if you knew how to leave and escape all consequences; I thought about having fun. I picked up a pink fondant fancy and bit it in half.

"My folks won't be back till late," Slightly grinned.

"That's nice."

"We could… go upstairs."

"I'm fine here thanks." And suddenly Slightly's hand was cupping my breast, a mischievous smirk on his face, "you enjoying that?"

"Are you?"

"No," I gripped his nipple and twisted.

"Ow! Why'd you do that?"

"Hands off Slightly."

"Don't call me that you know I don't like it."

"And I don't like being pawed, you touch me again and you'll be donating organs."

"You've changed your tune."

"A girl has the right to change her mind Slightly," I needed to buy time, I needed to work out a plan of action, my first challenge – outside of coping with Slater's amorous advances – was finding out who I was and where I actually lived, and I was with someone who clearly knew all the answers, all I had to do was get the information out of him, "let's get back to the books, get some studying done." I managed an hour of King Henry VIII and his relationship issues (seven wives – who the hell was Edith of Spain?) before I broached the issue, "what's my address?"

"Say what?"

"You heard me, you do know my address right?"

"Of course, I know your address."

"So, what is it?"

"What do you mean eyeeeah!" Slightly yelped like a kicked puppy – having a nipple sharply twisted anticlockwise will do that to you, "don't do that?"

"Answer my question Slightly."

"Don't call me that!" TWIST "Eeeeyah! Don't! Sixty-three Hillary Walk."

"And where's that exactly?"

"What?" TWIST "Owww! Stop it! I'll do it to you, se how you like it," Slightly reached for my breast and I slapped his face so hard I could see the red welt of my palm on his face.

Slightly's face was a cartoon of shock and indignation; his tastes were clearly less refined than my Slightly's, "you hit me!"

"I will do if you don't answer my question, where is Hillary Walk?"

"I don't get it, why..." I lifted my hand, "it's on Oakridge where it's always been, near the infants school."

That was as about as much information as I dared fish for; I felt an uncomfortable compulsion to justify my action, "Very good. See how that pain helped you remember something, now say King Henry."

"King Henry," TWIST "arragh! Will you stop doing that?"

"Concentrate! What is King Henry famous for?"

"Seven marriages, the English Reformation, creating the spilt from the Roman Catholic Church to marry Anne Boleyn, and the dilation of the…" TWIST "OW! Dissolution of the monasteries."

“Brilliant, there you go. Session over. Thanks for the cake. See you tomorrow.”

“You’re going? I thought we… you know… for a bit.”

“You thought wrong,” and to prove it, out the door I went.

There were only two ways of getting onto the Oakridge estate, through the underpass or over a bridge that spanned the dual carriageway. I decided to take the bridge just in case I was waiting to meet myself coming back.

Hillary Walk was a cul-de-sac made up of semidetached houses, something Popley didn’t possess, and a decade older than the 60’s London overspill project I lived on. This was the posh end of town; things were looking up. Number sixty-three turned out to be a semi with bay windows and a tidy little hedge around its tiny but trim front lawn. I walked up the path, put my key to the door – but it didn’t fit, why would it? I rang the bell, the chime sounded familiar. The door opened and there was…

“Mother?”

“Back so soon? Forget your key?”

“Mum,” I must have looked as stunned as I felt.

"Are you okay sweetie?"

"I… hi Mum. I didn't expect to see…" and there I was tearing up like a fool.

"Sweetie what's wrong, come on in," and there I was in a hug, with a woman who'd tried to kill me, "what's wrong? Tell me."

"Nothing… I'm just tired."

"Everything okay with you and Simon? Where did you get those shoes?"

I looked at my baseball pumps and shrugged, "they're Slightly's I borrowed them."

"Really? Hasn't he got small feet. Oh well, come in. How was Simon? I thought you were spending the evening revising," she led the way into the house, and although it was entirely different from my house, somehow it felt like home, "Sam, your daughter's home."

Father appeared out of the kitchen, a mug of tea in his hand, he looked great, he looked happy, "I thought you were spending the evening at Simon's."

"He had a headache, so I came back."

"Poor Simon. Are you hungry?" Mother asked.

“No thanks, I’m full of cake, I think I’ll …” what was I doing? “I’ll go up to my room.”

“Up? Don’t tell me we wasted all that money on the extension just so you can slum it upstairs in my office,” father laughed and sipped from his mug.

“Sam, she’s tired. You go right ahead sweetie., I’ll bring you a drink through.”

“Thanks, yeah, I think I need to… chill-out. I’ll see you guys later,” I stepped past father, and then turned to look at my mother’s smiling, breathing face, “looking good Mum, looking good.”

“Thank you, sweetie, I do try.”

“Very,” father grinned, “all the time, so trying” it seems dad jokes are the same no matter what reality you’re in.

I found myself in a spacious open plan kitchenet, with a small table set for two, with something that smelled delicious cooking on the stove – it occurred to me that I may have been ruining my parents evening, but I had more important issues to deal with than their date night – namely how to get to the bedroom, my bedroom. There were two matching wooden doors in the far wall. I turned to see father was watching me, his mug of tea locked into his face. I could feel my heartbeat striking up an alarming beat, and my hands were beginning to sweat. Something brushed against my legs and there was Wiggy, shaking his stub of a tail at me. I bent down and rubbed his aging head, "good lad, fooled you too ah."

"What was that?"

"Nothing Dad?" I had to get out of there before I blew it.

I picked the door on the left, it was a toilet, "need to pee," I stepped in and closed the door. My heart was racing, and the small room began pulsating in time with its rhythm – I sat on the toilet and tried to catch my breath. I needed to calm the fuck down, I flushed the toilet, splashed water on my face and opened the door, and there they both were, in each other's arms, grinning at me, "sorry, I just realised I've left something at Slightly's."

"Slightly? Slighty what?" Father mused.

"She means Simon darling, because he's Slightly…dull."

"He is that," father nodded, "I like it... Simon Ever-so Slightly Dull."

"Now look what you've done," mother said rolling her eyes at me, "you shouldn't call him that, I'm sure he wouldn't like it. I thought you liked Simon."

“I do, but… he is dull. Look, got to go, I don’t want to ruin your evening, so… I’ll be back later.”

“Can’t it wait till morning?” mum asked.

“Need a lift?” father was clearly much more focused.

“No, I’m fine,” I insisted, as I hurried to the door, “the walk will do me good.”

“Take the spare key,” Mum insisted opening a kitchen draw and removing a key on a heart shaped fob.

“What’s wrong with your key? Did you lose it?” father asked.

“Don’t fuss! She’s got a key that’s all that matters. Have fun sweetie, not too late now..” - I closed the front door behind me; my dead-not-dead mother’s voice ringing in my ears, I could fill the fire of emotions rising in my chest and it was going to make my head explode, I was going to choke on it. There was only one thing to do, I ran.

I ran to until the emotions had been drained from my chest and spiked my muscles, and I was panting steam and soaked through – and there I was back in the mouth of the underpass. I was also there, leaning against the wall waiting for myself.

"Been waiting long?" I asked myself.

"Where have you been?" I replied.

"Around, and you?"

"I went to my house, but I don't live there anymore," her eyes were sore from tears, "the world had completely changed, it was insane!"

"Did you meet Father?"

"No! I told you, I couldn't find my house. That is, I found my house, but I wasn't my house. I wasn't living there anymore! There was an old lady piano teacher living there, she thought I'd come for lessons."

"What did you do?" I had to ask.

"I learnt three bars of Janacek's The Cunning Little Vixen."

"Really?" I didn't know I could play piano, "and then what?"

"I came here and waited for you, what took you so long?"

"Well… like you said, I don't live where I used to live. It's a weird situation isn't it." I had to point out.

"Weird? It's horrible and I want it to stop. I want to go home, how do we put it right?"

"I don't know… but we could try crossing paths, see what happens. See if the world explodes this time."

"Still not funny, do you think you're funny? Is that your thing, being funny? Well you're not funny, you're weird and this whole situation is insane, and I want to go home."

As did I. But her spineless declaration rubbed salt into my contrary nature, and I heard myself say, "No. Not yet."

"What?"

"Look, I need six hours, six hours to look around and investigate, that's all I ask."

"Why?"

"I'm curious that's all... like you said, this is an insane situation, probably a totally unique situation, that's probably never happened ever before, and will never happen again. Don't we owe it to ourselves to look?"

"No, I'm not standing here for six hours."

"You don't have to, your address is fifty-six Chaucer, it's straight down that way," I tossed her my key.

"That's Simon's house?"

"No, it's yours, Slightly, I mean my Simon lives over on Streatfield, number seven or maybe eight, look you'll find it. Go to Chaucer Close, go to the top of the stairs, and it's the first room on your right, hide there all day if you like."

"No way."

"Or you could look around, look up Simon, wander around. Aren't you intrigued? Don't you want to see what being another you, in another world is like? Come on, we just walk away, and meet back here in six hours, at midnight. What's to lose? Six hours, till midnight, and then we all swap back no damage done."

"Is Sally alive in your world?"

"Horseface; I mean sure, Sally's there."

"Are we friends with Sally?"

"We are very good friends with Sally. She lives somewhere on Byron…"

"I know the address."

"You think you know the address," I pointed out.

"If she's there I'll find her."

“Great, so let’s do it, what harm can it do, six hours.”

My face grinned back at me, “alright six hours, I really do want to have a look around, but we meet back here at midnight, agreed.”

“Agreed.”

A house key skipped along the pavement towards me, and I picked it up. I couldn’t throw for shit. “See you at midnight.”

“See you at midnight,” I waved goodbye and watched her trot off into the estate, “midnight my arse.”

So where to start? It really didn’t matter, I had six hours to raise hell, placate my appetites, appease my needs, and have a whole lot of fun – and then I could get out of town, really out of town – at least one of me would. I had a smorgasbord of devilry ahead of me, and a world of straw houses waiting to be blown away; and I would huff, and I would puff and gather my little piggies in, slice by slice.

3

A row of semidetached houses lined either side of the road, they looked like dominos, waiting for me to send them toppling. I strode down that street feeling more powerful and hungry than I've ever felt. I wasn't afraid of the shadows, clutching my keys for safety or listening out for footsteps behind me; I was a proud predator ready to take whatever opportunity presented itself to me. I swear the soundtrack in my head was banging.

A silver car pulled up in front of a house just ahead of me, and a man in a shiny C&A grey suit got out, opened the boot, lifted a large white cardboard box on to the car's boot and slammed the boot shut. He then carried the box awkwardly, high up against his chest, with his keys in dangling from a finger, up the path towards the house.

"Here let me help you with that," I said running over and reaching for the box.

"It's okay, I can manage, its heavy love."

"Let me get the door for you," I took the keys and opened the door.

"Thanks very much love, appreciate that," his accent sounded Northern, only Northern's can say love and not make it sound creepy.

I stood back as he stepped through the door, "is there anybody in there to help you with that?"

"No, the Mrs is away till Wednesday, I'll put this in the kitchen," he did a short step rush, into the kitchen, and carefully placed the box onto a varnished wooden worktop with a sigh of relief. I stepped into the house, shut the front door behind me and followed him into the kitchen. It was a very nice kitchen, and I suspect recently renovated with a brand-new double hob cooker, a huge upright fridge, the kind you only saw those days in American sitcoms, and a very nice set of knives suspended on a magnetic board above a large stone chopping board, "nice kitchen."

"Cheers, we supply and fit them, one of the perks of the job...." and he proceeded to give me a five-minute tour of the kitchen which included specifications, building materials and prices; talk about stoking the fire, "...all top of the range, I'd have preferred a Lamborghini but that's another department right!" He laughed himself into an awkward pause.... "Anyway... thanks very much for the help pet, not many folks around here would do that. What can I get you? Can of pop? Glass of wine?"

“I’m too young to drink.”

“I won’t tell if you won’t, and like I said, I’ve got the house to myself tonight,” the leery wink really sealed the deal.

“Okay, a glass of wine would be great.”

“Great, I’ve got plenty,” he turned, opened the huge fridge, and lifted out a bottle of Blue Nun and set it on the worktop next to the cardboard box, it was like receiving a sign from the cosmos, “so how old are...” the leer dropped from his face when he saw me saw me grinning at him - fish knife in my hand, “what do you think you’re doing love? That’s sharp, put it down now before you hurt yourself...”

“I think you’re misunderstanding what’s happening here.”

“Put the knife down pet. Put it down and get out,” he grabbed the wine bottle and gripping it with both hands, like a baseball bat, “go on now, get the fuck out of my house!”

“Make me.”

He made a step forward, raising the bottle as he did so, demanding that I, “get the fuck out of my house you mad bitch…” I stepped forward and put the knife through his palm. The bottle fell to the floor and bounced away across the pale blue floor tiles. He reeled backwards, clutching his hand to his chest, eyes wide with alarm, "look what you've gone and done, you're for it now, you're fu..." – and I was on him.

I launched myself onto his shoulder, reached down his back and sunk the knife, hilt deep into his right kidney. As he dropped, I planted my feet on the ground, wrapped my arm around his throat, and put my mouth to his reddening ear, "you'll have to forgive me, but it's my first time, so this may not be as quick as you'd like…so what next? Between the shoulder blades I think, one, two and three." He slumped to his knees, blood spewing from his mouth. "So far, so good. Let's try for the other kidney, one, two, and just to be sure, three, four, five. How many is that all together, seven, eight? I've lost count. Let's make it a round, nine! Ten! This is a good knife, a good investment but I think I'm going to need something else now, wait there," he slumped to the ground as I released him.

I walked back to the magnetic knife rack, selected the black handled meat cleaver, raised it above my head and drove it down into his skull. He sunk into the floor like a wet rag. Silence, within and without, soundless utter stillness, a deep, satisfying calm. I took a minute or two to soak it in... bliss.

I washed the blood from my hands, helped myself to a can of Coke from the fridge, and drank it as I watched the pool of blood slowly creep along the blue floor tiles, creating a shimmering pearlescent vinier, that was as beautiful as any rose-tinted twilight. "I did that," I told myself, "I did that." My actions made that happen. I imagine that's how artists feel when they step away from their work and view it complete for the first time, "I did that, and I see that it is good." Looking back now, I think if I'd had a little more discipline, a little more self-control, I could have stopped there and been satisfied. But I was young and impetuous, and too much is never enough for the young. The cardboard box had shifted across the worktop; I must have caught it with my foot. I opened it up to find a large cake, grotesquely decorated in pink and pale green icing, across the centre of which was piped 'Happy Anniversary' – what an arsehole. I retrieved the bottle of Blue Nun from the floor and proceed to bash the cake into a pink pulp – too much is never enough.

I went out through the backdoor, through a bleak paved garden, and into a pristine back alley, and I remember thinking, "I really should have brought one of those knives with me," but you can't nip back to the scene when you're going on a rampage, it would completely spoil the whole point. A rampage is about moving forward, relentless forward motion, never looking back, not popping home to check you turned off the iron. And so, relentless, I moved forward.

4

And then I found myself back at the bridge that spanned the dual carriageway, not knowing how I got there. It seemed my idea of moving forward was to actually retrace my steps, and then I spotted an abandoned supermarket trolly, tipped up and cast aside into one of the coarse bushes the council used to fill odd patches of waste ground. I hate littering, it's really nothing more than vandalism. It does nothing but create an eyesore, and inconveniences everybody, littering is the panicle of antisocial behaviour, and I can't stand it. I pulled the trolley out of the bush and headed onto the bridge. Below me the car headlights were streaming along all four lanes, some going into town, others god knows where, little lit boxes full of purpose. I stood above the going out-of-town lane, watched the trucks and cars below me vying for position; and then hauled the shopping cart over the railings. There was a crash, the sound of breaking glass, a squeal of breaks followed by a metallic screeching of concertinaing metal, as one car rear-ended another, and another – the blare of horns – and then another screech, crumple, screech – I didn't even look down.

There's a park on the other side of the bridge, nothing fancy, but it's got some grand old trees that are older than anything else growing on the two estates. It used to be the grounds of the local manor house before the landowner, lord such and such, was dealt a compulsory purchase order, and the estates were built. It's a great place to hang out and read a book, as long as it's not filled with shouting shirtless football types, and it's always filled with shirtless football types. But at that time of night its usually occupied by dedicated casual drinkers, ardent young lovers and those that get off on watching ardent young lovers. I wasn't in the mood to watch but bagging two love birds with one stone sounded good, so I kicked around in the grass but couldn't find a suitably weaponised stone; thankfully a discarded beer bottle would do the job; littering is a dangerous business. I crept through the thickening shadows, listening for the deep moan or pleasured sigh that would bring me to my prey. I heard a giggle, somewhere off to my left, coming from the deep shadow of a spreading cedar tree. Crouching down, moving slow, I made my approach, and nearly fell over a fella stretched out on the ground.

"Shhhhh!" He hissed, raising a finger up to a weird pair of bulky goggles that were strapped to his face, "they'll hear you." And back he went to his intently pervy peering.

I figured the face-gear had to be some kind of night-vision googles; and was rather impressed; he was a well-prepared perve. What was I to do? Was chance offering me the opportunity to bag three birds with one bottle? But bashing one was likely to scare off the other two – on the other hand – foregoing one to take two would leave a witness, choices, choices, choices. But when you think about it, being a pervy peeping-tom is pretty low. The young lovers out there in the dark probably had nowhere else to go, and here was Mr Pervy Vision spying on their vulnerability – it wasn't right. I dropped my knees down onto his shoulders and with extended arms, out all my weight on the back of his head and pushed his face into the grass. He started kicking and screaming – although the screams were fairly muffled, there was no way the stalked lovers weren't going to hear him. Indistinct voices came from beneath the tree;

"What was that? I heard something, someone's there."

"Who's there? Who's there?"

"There better not be anybody there."

A muffled plea provided by my writhing victim proved, there was indeed, somebody there.

"Perve!" the male voice shouted defiantly.

"Let's get out of here," the other male voice directed.

Two birds flown, my plans blown, but I had one pigeon by the neck. I brought the bottle down hard on the back of his head. Once, twice and on the third blow it caught the edge of his binoculus and smashed. I rammed the jagged neck into the base of his spine and twisted. He jolted like an electric charge had passed through his body and then lay as still as a speed bump.

"Of all the things you could have done, you chose that," a very proper male voice intoned behind me.

In an instant, I was on my feet, bloodied bottle at the ready. A torch beam appeared at my feet, at the other end of the beam stood a middle-aged man, dressed in a thick overcoat and a flat cap, at his side was a raggedy looking mongrel on a choke-chain.

"What did you say?"

"I said, of all the things you could be doing with your time here, you chose to do that, what a waste of an opportunity."

“Excuse me?” The man a gave the dog’s lead a small tug and they both strode up to me as nonchalantly as if they were about to buy an ice-cream. “Don’t come any closer!” I snapped.

“Oh give over, I’m not going to hurt you. I could have done that while you were bashing in poor Harry’s head if I wanted to. That was Harry by the way, the person you just dispatched with such ease, poor old Harry.... I’m afraid he won’t be missed. None of us are, that’s kind of the point really.”

“What are you talking about?” I growled as I held the wet end of the bottle up to his face.

“You know exactly what I’m talking about. Did you really think you were the first to walk through that tunnel? Well, you’re not, not even close. Stay around here long enough you’ll see their lights, stay too long and you’ll become one.”

“What are you talking about? What lights? Who are you?”

The old man tugged twice on the dog’s choke chain as he turned his back on me and headed into the park, “come on I’ll show you, follow me.”

"I'm not following you anywhere!"

"That's up to you. Nobody's making you."

Running away would have made much more sense, but I'd already leapfrogged over sense and restraint – and if the worse came to the worse, I reckoned I could take the old guy without breaking a sweat, and his little dog too. So, I wiped my hands dry on my jeans, gripped the neck of the bottle, and followed the torch beam through the trees. We reached a circle of willow trees, that I knew surrounded a bullrush laden bog that was all that remained of the manor house's ornamental lake; it was a favoured place to dump old bikes and the occasional mattress – disgraceful behaviour. But on this occasion, the rushes were illuminated with a blood red glow that seemed to rise out of the waterlogged earth. The raggedy dog barked and immediately answered by a low rumble that came from the centre of the bog. I stepped forward and peered into the gloom, and there was the blood unicorn wallowing shoulder deep in the mire, munching on the bullrushes.

"Do you know what it is?" I heard myself ask.

"Not really, something ancient. It looks like a Elasmotherium to me, but what do I know?"

"Do what?"

“Siberian Unicorn, woolly rhinoceros.”

“It’s bald.”

“It’s old.”

“I used to think it was a blood unicorn.”

“And what is a blood unicorn?”

“That thing over there. Did you follow it here too?” it seemed like a reasonable assumption, “through the underpass?”

“I did. But the question is, was it the same underpass? Now that’s a real head scratcher isn’t it. Is there one plain of departure or are we many planes departing from many plains of reality? Look around you...”

I did, and I saw a multitude of lights, grey flickering lights moving in twisting, drifting circles beneath the trees. And then the lights became figures, dancing couples, and then lone figures, men and women, dancing unaccompanied, seemingly unaware of the other dancers, busily lost in their own circuit of the dance. In-between them strolled other figures, women in summer dresses, bustles, and corsets, miniskirts, bellbottomed jean and some, in next to nothing, whilst even more men in a multitude of uniforms and three-piece suits milled around them completely oblivious to their presence. Part of me wanted to run and get as far away from there as it was possible to get – back to the underpass and the real world if needs be; but the greater part of me was spellbound by the silent spectacle; it was coldly beautiful.

"Why is nobody talking?"

"I really couldn't say, I often wondered that myself, perhaps there's nothing to be said when you're stuck at the end of a disused line. Killing time for the killing time we had."

"What are you a fucking poet?"

The old man laughed, coughed up a clot of phlegm and spat at his dog, "that's a good one. I think I would have made a good poet, like Byron perhaps, a poet of perversity."

"And that's you is it? A pervert, is that what you do, spend your time perving out in the dark with your pervy friend?"

"No, we were very different animals, Harry liked to watch, he never hurt anybody, in some ways he was the most unobjectionable of the lot of us. You see we're all here because we chose to make the most of it when we came here, just like you did with Harry. This is where you come, when nowhere else will have you."

"Well. That sounds like bullshit to me," I'm not sure if I didn't believe it or just didn't like the sound of it, "and what about you? Why are you here?"

"That's easy, I like little boys. I've hurt plenty."

I took a step back and raised the broken bottle to his face, "you're a kiddie-fiddler. You're a fucking monster."

"Says the teenager who just caved in my best friend's skull. But, of course, you're right. I've come to realise the truth of it. I removed myself from my own world thinking I was doing the right thing, but all I've done is inflict myself on this world like a disease. I've spent half a lifetime here. I've gorged and consumed till I'm sick of it. But I can't stop feeding. I know what I am, and I despise myself."

"So you're feeling all redeemed, warm and cosy now are you?"

"Far from it. I'm not cured, because there's no cure for what I am. Once a monster, always a monster. But I am sick of it all. I wonder," the old man shone the torch into his own face, "would you be interested in doing this world a favour? A deal between one monster and another."

"I'm listening."

"Kill me. Put me out of my, and their misery. I feel I deserve to suffer, but nothing too prolonged if you don't mind, I think I'd panic and fight back, and I really don't want to hurt anybody else. You can keep my dog, or let him go, or kill him after you've done me, I don't really like him."

An oft repeated saying of my father's jumped into my mouth, "you know what the masochist said the sadist, 'beat me, beat me,' and the sadist said… no." The old nonce seemed to shrink in his disappointment, "but in your case; let the dog go, keep the chain."

He slipped the choke-chain from the dog's neck and put his boot to its arse, it shot off into the darkness without so much as a backwards glance.

"Give me that," I demanded reaching for the lead, he handed it over with a slight bow, "and would you mind removing your hat?" I placed the chain over his head and around his neck and led him to the small children's playground at the centre of the park; it seemed appropriate. I stood him against the bars of the climbing frame, tossed the lead over the top bar and stepped inside the frame, "last chance."

"Would you stop if I asked you to?"

"Probably not."

“Would you prefer it, if I put up a struggle?”

“I thought you didn’t want a fight.”

“I don’t. I was just trying to enhance the experience for you.”

“Nah, no need, it’s all the same to me. But if you don’t mind... what’s your name? I feel I should know.”

“Derek, Derek Compton, pleased to meet you.”

“Any last words Derek?”

“Just to say, I approve of the setting, it has some poetic symmetry.”

I pulled the lead taut, the choke chain tightened. It sounded like he was gargling with glass. I lifted my legs from the ground and swayed there suspended by the chain, as he too rose and kicked and kicked and kicked and then… no more paedo.

I put my feet down and released the chain; the body fell like a sack of shit. I felt the rising warmth of a job well-done, as if I’d just completed a really complicated flat-pack cupboard or put up a really straight set of shelves. A breeze stirred the tops of the trees, skeleton fingers rattling against the sky. The smell of damp pine needles and human excrement wafted through the air, as the grey lights of the silent dancers, and promenading ghosts wafted back and forth through the shadows. And then I saw Derek and peeping-tom Harry, standing together beside the seesaw, blank expressions on their faces, hands extended, pointing at me. I gave them the finger, what the fuck did they know. The grey lights went out, and the park fell into darkness.

I looked at the fallen body and suddenly realised, that in many people's eyes, I'd done a good deed. In fact, I'd actually carried out the perve's last wishes and protected the world from his violence - like I was a hero or something. Talk about a killing your buzz. I felt demeaned, my palate felt tainted – I needed a cleanser. Luckily there's a whole row of houses directly opposite the park, I walked up to the one with a bright red hunchbacked Fiat Panda parked on its front lawn. The sign beside the front door said:

NO CALLERS. NO HAWKERS.
NO SALESMEN. NO PILGRIMS.
NO PREACHERS. NO THANK YOU.

Obviously, I was obliged to knock. An old woman with a gravity defying bouffant pink rinse opened the door; "want do you? Can't you read!"

I grabbed her by the bouffant, pulled her head into the doorframe and slammed the door against it until she fell silent and her slimy dentures fell at my feet. I stamped on them and felt better. I pushed her back into the house and let the body fall to the floor; then shut the door behind me and stepped over her as I walked down the short corridor to the kitchen.

"Who are you? What are you doing in my house? Where's my wife?" An old geezer in a bib and a wheelchair barked at me.

"Give me a minute," I filled a glass with water and downed it.

"Who are you? Where's my wife? Margery! Margery! Who is this person! Margery!"

"Hold on Grandad I'll explain everything in a minute," I needed a second glass, I really was thirsty, "have you eaten? Pork chops was it? Sausages?" I said pointing to the old frying pan sitting on the hob.

"Margery! Margery who is this..."

Thirst quenched, I grabbed the frying pan and beat the old guy's head flat; it was proper heavy, well-made, probably cast-iron – it did the job. And when the job was done, the electric kettle boiled and clicked off, so I made myself a cup of tea and considered the scene. It was not pretty but in functional terms, as in getting from A to B, entering and dispatching the elderly residents, it had been flawless, seamless, a piece of precision engineering. I was getting good. I did consider looking through the old dears' stuff, having a quick mooch as it were, but I decided I didn't want to know; this way they were a couple of grumpy old folks trying to get by as best they could. If I snuck around, I might discover that he was an old Nazi and she was a baby killer, I didn't want that, I didn't want to justify my actions, my actions had been appalling. I wanted my violence to be clean, senseless and pure. A set of car keys were laying on the kitchen table, I picked them up, turned on all the stoves gas rings, shut the front door behind me and climbed into the Panda.

Now I'd never driven a car before, being too young to have lessons, but I knew the basics because my father had an incredibly annoying habit of talking through the procedure whenever he took our dull as fuck Nissan out for a ride. But it's not as easy as it looks, I got the car started without any bother, even managed to inch it off the front lawn and onto the road without much bother but made a right dog's dinner of getting down the road, a kangaroo in clown shoes couldn't have done a worse job. I eventually screeched it into second gear and there it stayed. As luck would have it, a furtive young couple were making their way out of the park and were about to cross the road, of course I made a bead for them, but the roar of the engine and my lack of speed gave them plenty of warning, and they made their escape back into the estate with raised fingers expressing their dissatisfaction with my driving technique. I was no more than half a mile down road when the engine started pouring out smoke and I had to stop. I was climbing out of the thing when a Ford Cortina pulled up behind me.

"Engine trouble," a lanky sod in a loose-fitting white t-shirt asked, as he climbed out of the car, "want me to have a look?"

"Would you mind? I really don't understand cars. I'm a girl."

He chuckled to himself and swaggered to me, "pop the hood love, let's have a look see."

Hood? Where did he think he was Kansas? I had no idea how to "pop the hood," but I made a good show of looking around – then decided to fall back on; "oh I'm such an idiot, I can't remember where it is. I'm such a girl."

"It's on the left-hand side love," he called out; then opened the passenger door, reached in and did it himself – he looked a guy who did a lot for himself, and often.

"It's my mum's car. I don't really know it. I was just picking it up for her. She's in the hospital," I added just for colour.

"Nothing too serious I hope," he feigned as he opened the bonnet. A cloud of smoke billowed into his face, "Jesus, that's not good," he coughed – and I decided to take my chance. My karate chop was aimed at his throat, but the smoke was thick, my aim bad and basically, I'm four inches too short for such a move. I connected with his stony sternum, and damn near broke my little finger. But it still winded him, he stumbled sideways, scrambling like stilt walker trying to keep his balance and then came back swinging. The lanky bastard had no style or coordination but a long reach and caught me just above my left eye. Stars swirled, and I felt my knees begin to buckle, but I'd taken a hit or two in the Popley dojo and knew how to gather myself and reset - it felt good to have someone fight back. He stepped in to deliver a punch, but I threw myself at his chest and sunk my teeth in deep. He tried to push me away, grabbing a fist full of my hair trying to pull my teeth from his bleeding chest, but I pushed forward, and he fell backwards onto the hot engine. He screamed in panic and finally managed to shove me, aside but as he staggered from the car, I launched myself from its wing - knocking him to the ground. I clambered on top of him twisting my thumb deep into his eye, and my knee into his groin. He rolled away groaning, formed a protective foetal ball, arms up over his head, and lay there sobbing. Winded and a little shaken I made my way to the Fiat's boot, there was a woollen blanket, an empty flask, a five litre plastic green petrol can – half full, an aluminium walking frame and a wooden walking stick.

"No more, please, no more," Mr Lanky wheezed as he rolled onto his knees and began crawling towards his car.

I decided to delay his journey with a running kick to stomach, he collapsed into the grass, rolling back into his protective ball, "no more please, no more"

"Will you shut up, I'm trying to think."

"Please no more, no more, what have I ever do to you."

"Done to me? Done to me, it's not about me. It's about you, it's about, smile babe it suits your face, it's about cheer up love might never happen. It's about, get your tits out!"

"It wasn't me! I've never seen you before!" he protested.

“That’s not the point, you’re symbolic, the handsome prince, coming to rescue the helpless princess!”

“I was only trying to help!”

“I said, its symbolic!”

I marched back to the car, took the walking stick from the boot, broke it in half under the wheel trim, and drove both shafts through Mr Lanky’s neck. His blood swiftly drowned his cries for help. I stood over his body waiting for someone to respond to the commotion; but nothing stirred. No one noticed. I laid him out straight, took the handbrake off the Fiat, and rolled it forward, concealing the body. I’m not sure why I bothered but it was easier than trying to get the lanky bastard back in the car. I did think about taking the Cortina but decided against it, on the grounds that only tossers drive Cortinas.

Five hundred yards away, across a threadbare strip of grass that splits the estate in two, stood a true example of brutal-as-fuck architecture: the Popley maisonettes – all gone now. They were buildings so inhumane they could’ve only been designed by a committee of alien insectoids or middleclass know-alls. House stacked on house supported on stilts linked by mid-air walkways that oozed slime when it was dry and ran with black rivers when it rained. They were an afront to my eyes. The clock in the car said it had just gone ten, two hours to midnight, time enough to start a fire. I took the petrol can from the Fiat's boot and headed off to prep the barbeque.

The maisonettes had communal bins, big grey metal tin cans on wheels, which they stored in the carpark beneath the maisonettes, just so the rats had easy access. They'd always looked like outsized cooking pots to me, and I was sure they'd make first rate braziers. There were three of the beasts, I poured most of the petrol into one and then emptied the rest onto a nearby ripped foam mattress that was leaning on the wall behind them. It would make a lovely start – if I could light it, which it suddenly occurred to me that I couldn't. I don't smoke and I'm not the sort of person who casually carries around a lighter or a box of matches just in case someone asks for a light or needs to be turned into a Roman candle. I was kicking myself for being an idiot, when a gruff male voice blurted behind me; "Wot you doing there?"

I turned to see Boosey, replete in string vest and bother-boots bearing down on me, "I said wot you doing?"

"Nothing?"

“Nothing. It don’t look like nothing. You look like you’ve been in a fight.” He clocked the petrol can in my hand and narrowed he’s already piggy eyes. “Wot you doing with that? You trying to start a fire?” – what an intellect.

Why lie? “Yes, I wanted to get rid of this mattress it won’t fit in the bin.”

He stepped forward, snatched the petrol can from me and threw it across the carpark, “don’t be a fucking idiot. You any idea how toxic that smoke would be?”

I had a pretty good idea, but he didn’t need to know that; “no, really, is it?”

“Of course it fucking is, that’s foam that is, now go on get out of it before I give you a thick ear.”

I really didn’t think I can handle another fight, and certainly not one with Boosey, so I shrugged and turned to go.

“Hold on a minute. Where did you say you lived? Which number?” I paused too long. “You don’t live round here do you, what’s your game then, trying to start fires under other people’s houses.”

"Oh, go suck dick Bossey," I spat and ran, and Boosey came after me. I'll say this for him, for a big fella with no neck he could certainly shift over short distances.

"Bobbie! Charlie! Over "ere!" I heard him shout, and suddenly there were three of them after me. People appeared on the walkways and started cheering, pointing at me as I cleared the carpark and headed into the maze of darkened back alleys. I didn't know that side of the estate as well as my own, but I knew if I could crisscross down through the back alleys, I would reach home turf, and then they'd never catch me, all I had to do was make it across the road. I ran the length of three blocks, took a sharp left, run across a small concrete playground, and then headed down the road, but they were still on my heels. Now I had a choice, break for the road or take a sharp left and go for another underpass that would take me under the road and back into the park. Getting caught in an underpass didn't sound smart. I sprinted for the road, but the dogs were soon at my heels. I saw a light coming down the road, at first, I thought it was a motorbike and then I could see it was a car, one headlight was blown the other was dimmed to almost nothing. I had to time this right or I was buggered. I ran into the road, and headed straight for the one coming car, Boosey and his mates (Bobby and Charlie) followed suit. In a split-second I heard mu pursuers behind panicked cries, saw the driver's terrified face and the stars in the night sky blur as I threw myself out of the car's path. The car's brakes screeched as it collided head-on with Boosey smearing him across the road, before side-swiping Charlie (possibly Bobby) crushing him against the curb and taking out a lamppost. Bobby – possibly Charlie – stood on the other side dry heaving at the sight of the Boosey glazed tarmac at his feet. I walked up to him, kicked him in the balls, and then delivered a flawless roundhouse Mawashi Geri to his head. He dropped, face down, deep in Boosey.

"What happened, is everybody alright, did I hit somebody?" the driver of the car recited as he crawled out of the smashed windscreen and wobbled precariously to his feet, "is everybody okay? They just came out of nowhere... I didn't have a chance."

"Oi, Carlos Fandango, you dropped something?" I shouted.

He looked at me with the attention of a punch-drunk boxer in the tenth round, "what? Say what was that?"

"You're missing something," I pointed.

He looked behind him, "my car, my car's fucked."

“Not that bright boy. Look again,” I pointed to my shoulder.

He looked at my shoulder and then to his own, and “my arm, my arms gone! Where’s my arm gone?”

“Don’t worry you should be joining it any time now...”

“Time...” he looked at his watch, which was still attached to his attached arm, which was handy, “nearly eleven o’clock, you’re welcome... where’s my arm?” he swayed on the spot, mouth open, white as that often sited white sheet, and then fell to the tarmac with a thud that I felt in my back teeth. I checked his wristwatch – he was right, it was eleven.

5

I was tired, thirsty and every joint and bone ached. It was only eleven o’clock but my time was up. I felt sated. I had had my fill. Well, just about, on the way to my underpass rendezvous, there was a late-night store, I knew I could make it in ten minutes and have time to spare. But I jogged, just to be sure; I arrived sweaty and panting, like a marathon runner with asthma, I walked in, took a beer off the shelve, cracked it and downed it.

“Hay you, you can’t do that? You got any I.D? You’re going to pay for that,” the wire-haired biddy with gull-winged specs bawled at me from behind the cash register.

“I can’t, I don’t have any money and I’m underage. It’s illegal to sell me any beer. Have a nice evening,” I grinned and made for the door.

“No, you don’t Miss, pay up or we’ll see what the police have to say about this,” a dumpy meat sausage in latex cycling gear blocked my path and put his finger in my face. He had that self-assurance and presence that comes from being a middle-aged man who’s never listened to a word anybody else had ever said – yes, a total wanker.

I smiled, curtsied, took a step forward and put my knee in his well stuffed groin. He took two steps backwards, fell into the shelving and rolled into a ball. I picked up a fallen tin – I think it was readymade custard, but I can’t be sure – and drove its edge into his face, until I my arm ached, and his face resembled a crushed cherry pie. The gull-winged specs behind the till screamed and at least three shoppers fled from the store – taking their unpaid produce with them no doubt. But what did I care about witnesses? I had an exit plan. As I made my way to the underpass, I heard sirens coming from all directions. Lights were turning on in upstairs windows, people opened doors to see the commotion, and behind me the gull-winged specs were screaming, “she’s getting away, stop her, stop her, she’s getting away.”

She was right but nobody did. I reached the underpass with five minutes to spare. I threw myself into the piss stinky tunnel, gasping for breath, not from effort but from laughter, I’d never felt so good. The agony of wanting was gone. I’d eaten my fill and felt like I would burst. As the cold damp of the paving began to impede on my joy, I readied myself for the journey to come. I got up, brushed myself down and - still unable to staunch my giggling – tidied my hair, with three minutes to go. An unseen police car sped across the road above me, its siren wail whipped through the tunnel and whirled off into the night, two minutes to go and still no hue and cry, no posse, no lynch mob, no way to stop me, one minute till midnight.

Midnight came and despite being there myself I was still absent. I called out into the darkness; “are you there?” I didn’t answer. No one answered. Ten minutes later and I was pacing, fifteen minutes later I was bouncing off the walls. I wasn’t coming. What kind of irresponsible, unreliable arsehole was I?

I was a fool ever to trust myself. Perhaps something had happened? Had she done the same as I and been caught? Had she had an accident? Had she been murdered? What the fuck did it matter?! I wasn't there, and now I was stranded there – what a bitch. At one thirty, I made my way home.

I let myself in, crept through the front room and kitchen and went into "my room." I turned on the overhead light to see the wall above the bed covered with photos and hand drawn pictures of Sally, horse-faced Sally. Smiling like a horse-faced angel. There were photos of Sally and I sitting side-by-side, are arms entwinned, strips and strips of grinning passport photos, our heads pressed close together – it was sweet and utterly nauseating. I slumped down onto the bed and saw something sticking out beneath the pillow. It was a scrapbook, completely empty but for three newspaper clippings;

LOCAL GIRL MURDERED

ARREST OF LOCAL MAN

LIFE FOR THE MURDER OF LOCAL GIRL

And each headline had the same picture of Horse-Faced Sally gurning into the camera like a horse-faced clown, alongside the usual tagline, "Much missed, valued member of society, a sweet spirit, a senseless loss," and alongside the last was another picture, a mugshot of the convicted Harold Pole, local pensioner and guineapig breeder. The pieces fell together. “that two timing, swinging bitch. She was playing Slightly.”

And there was I thinking I was the evil doppelgänger; ever felt like you’ve been had?

6

I awoke fully dressed, feeling like I hadn’t slept. The mocking laughter and knowing looks from the bastards on the walls had been too much to bear. I could hear voices talking in the kitchen and got up to face them.

“Morning sweetie, good night? Breakfast?” Mother asked.

“No, I’m late. I need to get to Slightly’s.”

“I do wish you wouldn’t call him that, he can’t like it,” she scolded, “and you need to eat something, take some toast.”

“Did you hear those sirens last night?” Father asked, teacup in hand.

“No, not a thing,” Mother replied, “what was it? Fire engines?”

"Not sure, might have been, there were lots of them, it was a real row. Did you see anything?" he asked looking at me.

"I think something happened at the shop on Oakridge Road. I might have seen an ambulance."

"Oh dear, I hope nobody was hurt," Mum winced.

"If there was an ambulance, somebody got hurt," Dad observed.

"You know what I mean," Mum retaliated with a fake glare that ended in a grin – which Dad return with a wink - somebody had got lucky last night.

I left the house with a slice of buttered toast in my hand, and made my way back to the underpass, praying I'd meet myself coming back, but when I was there, the cupboard was bare. I waited in the stink until the dank air and frustration had me drudging back home in a furious fug. What a fool I was to think I could be trusted, and yet I couldn't really blame myself – I hadn't asked why I was so keen to see Horse-faced Sally, and if I was in her place would I have done anything different? But then again, I was in her place, and she was in mine, the conniving bitch. I'd been had by myself, and not in a good way. When I got home, mother was weeping on the couch, father was standing in a corner visibly shaking, and D.S Sims and three heavyset police officers were waiting.

I was taken to the local copshop, where procedure and protocol were followed, none of which is worth recalling I was searched, logged in, and placed in a cell for six hours. I was informed of my rights several times, and assigned legal counsel, a Mr Cecil Todds, a stiff man of formal and proper baring, who seemed to stiffen with ever question I answered.

"I would remind my client she is talking under caution," he would say, and when we were alone "I would remind you young lady that you have the right to silence, use it." But why would I? I could not deny the presence of witnesses and why should I deny my actions? A murderer I may have been, a liar I was not. However, when it came to my account of the underpass, the blood unicorn and the dancers in the park I saw Mr Todd and Sims exchange glances, and Todd seemed to gather some of his former composure.

"I think my client is in need of a psychiatric assessment," he pronounced, "and I would insist this be carried out before any further questions are put to her, as I fear my client's mental state maybe undermining the validity of her statements."

“Your client seems very well aware of events,” D.I Sims snarled, “I have no reason to doubt her capacity at his time.”

“Indeed, however I am not questioning her capacity to answer questions at this time, I am questioning her capacity at the time of the alleged incidents, the same time she was seeing unicorns and ghost dancers in the local park.”

“Had you taken any substances prior to these events,” Sims asked me.

“I would remind my client, she under caution and is not obliged to answer that question,” Todd intoned mechanically.

“No, I hadn’t taken anything, I don’t do drugs. You can do a blood test it you like,” I’m not sure who looked more surprised Todd or Sims.

“We may very well do that,” Sims purred, “just to make sure the question of capacity is settled.”

“The question will not be settled until she is examined by a mental health professional,” Todd insisted, with the politest sneer I have ever seen.

There was of course no fault with my memory or my mind – but I’m not so dumb as to not see a door when it opens before me, “I must say I am feeling a little confused by recent events, you know I have seen unicorns before, I followed one to the underpass the other day, and then it just disappeared, very odd" I offered.

I could almost hear Sims' blood boiling.

And so, my introduction to psychiatry began. I spoke with two different consultant psychiatrists over the next month on four different occasions, all whilst on remand at Rampton Hospital in Nottinghamshire – which is nowhere near my hometown, so visits from mater and pater were few and far between, but I didn't mind. If anything, being out of their reach made the experience easier to bear; at least that way I didn't have to deal with the emotional pain and distress they were carrying – which I found tedious, and also very hard to witness. My placement posed a significant issue to the authorities, given my age I was a Young Offender, but I wasn't yet convicted, so needed to be held on remand and yet I was deemed too dangerous to be held with the Y.O's system without significant medication – which they couldn't give me because I was also suspected of having an undiagnosed psychotic disorder with homicidal tendencies, which they needed to rule out – which they couldn't do if I was actually treated for the condition they thought I had; the treatment being a chemical cosh that would reduce all but the strongest souls to jellyfish. However, this probable diagnosis did mean I required a level of care and observation not provided in adult detention centres, and that's why they sent me to Rampton which had a secure hospital wing and staff who could determine if I was faking it or not. That being said, they could have sent me to Broadmoor, which has the same setup and was closer to home, but I think that element of their decision making was probably fuelled by spite.

It was a fascinating experience. The staff were exceptionally attentive, they asked questions, and I answered them, and they listened, and I mean really listened, I can see why such things could become addictive. To be the centre of attention with no physical claim made on you but your time? It's a unique experience and one I would thoroughly recommend to anyone facing life in jail for mass murder.

Once again, I told the whole thing, from beginning to end and left out no detail. I saw no reason to lie but also no reason not to play their game and so told the tale with some relish. And again, and again I was asked, "do you believe you know the difference between right and wrong," I answered truly, "I believe I do, but I do believe they are subjective positions created to bind and control society, but if what the Prime Minister says is true, 'that there is no such thing as society,' what does it matter? If there's no society, how can there be societal rules." I was an obnoxious arse.

I was also repeatedly asked about my relationship with my mother, whom I insisted was dead, and they claimed was alive, "no that's not my mother, it looks like my mother but she's an alternative version. But she seems very nice?"

"Why do you say your mother is dead?"

"Because we buried her seven years ago, if she's not dead, she's bloody furious that's for sure."

And why shouldn't I play the mad card, what had I to lose? There are certain benefits to being a notoriously dangerous lunatic which I would never had access to in prison. Most importantly, a room of my own, and I had other privileges than I would not have expected, for example I didn't have to wear prison clothing, Levi's supply free clothes to mental institutions, did you know that? I was allowed reading materials, and visitors who were allowed to bring me in food. But the guards made it clear to me that this last point was an exceptional privilege and not the rule, and should I be very cautious about claiming it. I had no wish to encourage visitors for the sake of food, so rarely bothered the guards with such claims, but on the few occasions my not-parents visited, I made sure they brought chocolate bars, which I could then trade for favours from the other inmates – more of that soon.

At my hearing my barrister made much of my damaged mental health, and so he should that's his job; "the loss of Miss Kent to a violent death caused my client significant and lasting distress, and so damaged her psyche, that this normally caring and conscientious young girl, was driven to acts of homicidal rage, that are quite contrary to her nature." Sounded good to me, and I think the judge bought it too, but there was no way I was going to walk away from such heinous crimes. They had a real smorgasbord to choose from, including six counts of first-degree murder, three counts of manslaughter, five counts of reckless endangerment – that was the shopping trolley incident, two attempted arsons – that's the maisonette bins and gas in the house that didn't ignite – grand larceny, that's the car theft - and one count of shoplifting, I'm kidding, they didn't pursue the shoplifting. Whatever they finally decided to run with, I was looking at serious time, no two ways about it. The only question was where? A prison, or a hospital for the criminally insane? And despite the single room and new denim-wear, I can assure you that a secure mental health hospital is not an easy option. It's true that many people in prison should be in hospital, but you wouldn't want the people in hospital in prison, and certainly not in a prison cell with you. Three months into my stay at Rampton I had to face a hearing, to decide whether or not a I was fit to plead, and the judge, I can't recall his name, old fella, looked like a wilted Cornish Pasty with all the filling sucked out; he wanted to see me for himself, he wanted to be sure, I wasn't trying to pull a fast one, and so I was called to testify to my own sanity.

To start with I confessed to everything. I even admitted to killing my stepmother Gladys and the scheme with the guineapigs, which my barrister informed the judge was a fabrication of my disordered mind and had never happened and could not have happened as I'd never had a stepmother and both my parents were both still alive. I then told them about the blood red unicorn that might have been a Elasmotherium, and my ability to travel from one reality to another to another via a piss stained underpass – why hide it? Both my visiting psychiatrists gave evidence, and both agreed that at the time of my crimes I was in the throes of a previously undiagnosed delusional disorder and experiencing an acute psychotic break. In their opinion I was non compus mentus prior, during and post event; the term used by one psychiatrist was 'bone mad' deep down irrevocably insane. My father gave evidence in my defence. He blamed himself for not seeing the signs, for not taking the loss of Sally Kent more seriously. He insisted I was acting out of character, that I was a loving daughter, a good and honest person, which prompted me to shout out, "not honest enough to keep a promise and show up when I said I would is she!" which was a little showy, but I think by that point I was pushing on an open door when it came to the question of my mental state.

A psychologist I have no memory of meeting prior to the hearing suggested that my obsession with Mr Pole's guineapigs was in some way an allusion to the trauma Mr Pole had inflicted upon me by murdering my sweetheart, Sally Kent. As justifications went it seemed pretty lame to me, but nobody was asking my opinion at that point, I was just a bit player in their play; so I let them get on with it. I discovered court wasn't really about justice but about society seeing justice done; I'd already admitted to the crimes, what else did they require of me? If it had been about giving the friends and families of my victims a platform to express their loathing of me, I would have been all for it; but this was the 80's and the judicial system wasn't interested in such paltry peripherals as friends and family. The court had a job to do, and it was going to do it cold, blind and as clinically as possible. So the outcome was thus; I had committed the crimes I was accused of, but I was not sane prior to or during those deeds, so could not be held accountable for them. However, I was too ill and too dangerous to be let loose in society. So instead of a life tariff of say twenty-five years (which means being eligible for parole after twenty-one years), I was held on a Section 41 – which means if I was ever to be released, the Minister of Justice would have to sanction it. To put it in simply, the door was locked, the key lost and the person in charge of the lock, had no desire to find it.

Father cried, mother cried, and strangers booed – nobody was happy with the outcome. I cannot honestly say how I felt, because by then, I was stoned out of my tiny mind on their medicinal drugs – chemical coshed to the max! What I saw from that dock on that final day was a herd of inflated marshmallow people trying to sieve sunlight through balloon words that floated from the top of their marshmallow heads – completely off my box, but the truth wasn't any saner, I was an alien prisoner in an alien world that I could not convince I was an alien. The fundamental truth was that I had done what they said I'd done, if not for the reasons they thought – what was there to do but get on with it?

7

And back to Rampton I went. The brief incarceration that followed was not without incident, how could it be, collecting mad frogs in a box is a well-known recipe for disaster. I shared a wing – not a ward but a wing – with ten other girls, I used the term girl's because that's how we referred to ourselves and how we were treated. The entirety of our waking days were organised and our nights were spent behind locked doors. We were fed and watered, occupied and distracted by order, routine and a strict medication regime. Personally, I've never had a problem with routine, I find holding to a strict regime oddly liberating, as it tends to give you more time to think; but I don't like distraction, I don't even like the word. It makes me feel like I'm in a BBC Jane Austin adaptation; "Is something wrong Miss Pumbleton-Smyth, you're looking terribly distracted today?"

"How kind of you to enquire Mr Whythering-Dick-Stropper, and I fear your observation is correct, I am distracted, terribly so, but what else could a young woman be when confronted by the unsightly bulge in your tight breaches Mr Whythering-Dick-Stropper?"

The institutional meaning and intent of distraction could be stated as; occupation devised to burn time, or the awareness of the passing of time. Many people develop hobbies when they're inside – jigsaw puzzles, exercise, building cathedrals out of dried snot - but very few would follow the same course if they weren't locked-up, it's just something to do. I find that level of self-deception difficult to maintain, unless I'm truly interested in the subject, such a karate or wallfish. And that's where the drugs/medication comes in handy, they're not actually trying to treat you when you're inside, they're trying to subdue and sedate you – and I was all for that.

Two haloperidol in the morning, followed by two in the evening with a 5mg dose of procyclidine to ward off the side-effects, suited me very nicely. I did have a couple of excursions into the land of thioridazine and chlorpromazine, but I'll leave that stuff for the plebs – haloperidol all the way for me. I have no idea if 'Old Hal' as it was known, is actually any good at treating what it's meant to treat – psychosis – because I'm not psychotic, but I can tell you, that if you're in your right mind or not, it hits you harder than three brandies for breakfast – brilliant stuff,

The main reason I didn't mind taking 'Old Hal,' wasn't the period of incarceration but the people I was locked-up with, we were a horrible box of frogs. There was Tina Morris a walking misspelt tattoo with halitosis and a sexually transmitted skin rash that meant she paid more attention to her crutch than a nervous two-year-old boy. Tina's entire lexicon entirely composed of inane phrases as; 'you know what I mean like, play the white man, that's how it is like, and like a duck to water,' the last of which is a perfectly reasonable response in the right situation, but not really applicable to every cup of tea, every voluble passing of wind and every tampon utilised for its appropriate function. Let's put it like this, we weren't ever going to be bosom buddies, no matter how long we spent together. And yet... we were going to spend the rest of our lives together. Tina was the foul result of a foul life. She'd been abused by virtually every male member of her family as a matter of course and then prostituted by her drughead mother to every drug dealing scumbag in the Midlands. This of course led her to form her own legendary habit, which so addled what was left of her traumatised mind that went she finally turned on her abusers, she went a tad to far and ended up walking down a busy high-street carrying two severed heads, screaming; "it's the bloody Jews that done it." Tina was never going to cured, Tina was cooked – and according to the psychiatrists we were all in the same pie with her.

Joining me in the pie of despair, my other 'wing mates;' were three husband killers (two poisoners, one stabber), and three child killers, one of which had cooked two of her children in an oven, whilst the other two had suffocated theirs, one on Christmas morning and the other on Mother's Day. And then we had two notorious, and now aging murderous children, one who had killed another child and one who had gutted both her parents, her name was Pearl, and I was rather fond of Pearl. She had the presence of a dust-bunny and the demeanour of a shy librarian, but the temper of a panther with tooth ache. I once saw her nearly bite through an orderly's thumb for serving her mashed potato that was touching her peas. How could you not warm to such a soul? The other 'killer child;' Emily, I didn't care much for, she'd established a prison wing marriage with Jean, an arsonist who'd partially cooked herself when she set fire to the Catholic boarding school she'd been raised in; she looked like a weird combination of marble cake and wax work figure – but Emily loved her. The authorities had turned a blind eye to their relationship, and Emily and Jean's credit it was ten years on and going strong; although they liked to spice up their relationship every now and then by becoming murderously jealous and accusing each of other of being a slag or a slut with someone else on the wing, or failing that, a prison guard – both of these options were utter tosh, nobody else wanted a slice of that cake; merely greeting one was to risk the wrath of the other – I just didn't have the energy for such soapbox drama. I was haloperidol heavy, bone tired.

Dreams are what you escape into in captivity, I know why the caged bird snores. And at first, I found this a very entertaining pursuit, but as the drugs in my system continuously shouldered their way through my blood brain barrier my dreams became grey and insipid and about as entertaining as cold porridge.

I mentioned this during one of my weekly sessions with a psychologist – a well-spoken but exceptionally thin Welsh woman named Alison, that we were all convinced had an eating disorder or was dying of cancer – and it was she that enlightened me to the role medication was probably having on my dreams. At first it was an exchange I was willing to make, grey cold porridge days for grey cold porridge nights, but soon I began to have difficulty differentiating daytime from sleep time, and to compensate spent longer and longer periods of time in total silence. This soon leached into my family's visits, my therapy and group sessions, and before I knew it, I hadn't spoken in three months. But nobody professional complained, why should they, I was the perfect inmate. I walked from here to there. I sat in that chair until I was told to sit in another chair. I ate and I washed. I wasn't in anybody's hair, doing nobody any harm and had nothing to say. I'm sure it would have gone on like this until the end of my days had it not been for a scrawny little twat called Susie Binks.

Susie was a self-generated psychotic; sniffing the gas from caravan gas cylinders will do that to you; great swarths of his brain had turned to mush and the rest was just bitch. When medicated she lived in a minimal existence within a constant repeating loop that consisted of stand, sit, stand, light cigarette, inhale, check wrist (no watch), inhale, check wrist (still no watch), exhale, check watch (hadn't had a watch in years), inhale, (what time is it?) exhale, drop cigarette butt, sit, stand and repeat… and repeat. And this was her being well. But being that well was making Susie very sick and had reduced her lungs to something a hardened smoker in their seventies could have expected; but when the staff tried to control her smoking, she became uncontrollably violent and needed to be heavily sedated and locked in a padded cell for the night. If Susie approached you for a cigarette, you either handed one over, called for help or repeatedly told her you didn't smoke, until the information finally sank in, or she attacked you . I did not smoke, Susie saw I didn't smoke and I didn't feature in her world view, but then one unseasonably hot afternoon in Easter, I was sitting in the corner of the activities room, spaced out of my tiny mind. When a nicotine craving Susie approached and demanded, "give me a cigarette," and I didn't reply, I didn't know I hadn't replied, I'm not sure I knew how to reply at that juncture, and so we just kept looking at each other, with Susie's demands of "give me a cigarette," becoming more and more agitated. By rights, staff were meant to oversee our time in the activity room and should have intervened – that didn't happen until it was way too late.

The next thing I know, I'm on my back, and Susie is jumping up and down on my chest. As the (un) attending guards pulled off and dragged her away. I began spitting blood. I had a shard of white bone sticking of my chest, and it felt like I was drowning.

I was rushed (airlifted actually) to Queens Medical Centre in Nottingham, but I can't say that I remember anything about it or the following week, due to be placed in a medical induced coma. The next week is pretty foggy too, thanks to a nasty staphylococcus infection that saw me transferred to a corner of the hospital, with my own nurses and a rotating schedule of three guards – Georgina, a butch lesbian from Trinidad, Wioletta, a butch lesbian from Dansk, and Victoria, a butch non-lesbian from Harrow. If you're expecting a grand escape, with a clever bit of showboating involving a riot or a fire alarm, I'm sorry to disappoint you. I had no intention of escaping because I had no intent. My will was broken, along with my chest. In the end it all came down to chemistry. I was in a lot of pain, which required a lot of top-of-the-line analgesics, which couldn't be used in combination with my usual meds for fear of suppressing my already compromised respiratory system, so my medication regime was altered to preserve my life – and the dreaming began.

I was another; standing on a vast undulating grassy plain. The moon in the crystal saturated sky glows red but has never looked colder. I can see a long procession of skin clad figures walking away from me. I'm being left behind. I don't have the strength to follow. I know if I shout, they'll come and get me. I need to shout, but I can't open my mouth. My lips are frozen shut by the icy wind that ripples the grass and gnaws at my nose. I try to follow, I need to keep up but my feet won't move, I'm going to be left behind, abandoned to an icy fate. And then I see it, rising up out of the grass, a huge horned beast that glows red as it reflects the cold moonlight. It sees them, I try to shout, to warn them, but I can't speak. I see the beast lower its head and charge. It charges along the line, smashing them down one after another; bludgeoned, battered and torn the survivors try to scatter but the beast turns back and ploughs them down, crushing and goring all in its path. I see my mother trying to crawl away. A nudge from the beast's nose spins her onto her back. It places a foot on her head and crushes it like an egg. And still it's not done; slowly and purposefully it moves from one wailing survivor to another, and stomps them into the dirt, until there is nothing left but the sound of its own snorting. And still, I can't move. It sees me, slowly, ponderously, its massive, bloodied horn swinging, it approaches; closer and closer and still I cannot move. Its breath is hot and grassy on my face. Its skin like jagged stone. But it does not hurt me – it knows me, it recognises me as its own. It turns and walks away, my feet are unlocked, I could run but I have no need to run, I am with my own, I follow on. The beast leads me to an earthbound cloud hidden within the tundra. It enters the cloud and sinks into the muddy bog beneath the rising steam. I watch it wallow, horn deep in the mud. I throw off my furs, and step in, I sink down into the warming, soothing mud, I am where I belong, one thought rises with the steam, I need to get home.

A three weeks later I overhear a young medic talking with one of my guards, Georgina from Trinidad. He's ordered an MRI scan and if that proves, as he expects, that I'm healing well and free of any further complications, I'll be on my way back to Rampton at the end of the week. I take the news lying down, I don't have much choice, as I'm handcuffed to the bed. A few hours later an orderly arrives to take me to the Radiology Department but as I'm being wheeled down the hall, Georgina in tow, a nurse in a blue uniform snatches the notes at the end of the bed, flicks through them, and then tells the porter wheeling my bed to wait, as she calls down the corridor for a doctor. Another medic arrives, he's slightly older than the last so I take it he's superior to the former, and when he views the notes, he tuts, and scrawls something across the bottom of the page. The nurse, very kindly explains to Georgina that I can't have an MRI because I have metal pins in my chest and so it will have to be a CT scan, Georgina nods along as if she's understood every word – I imagine she's spent twenty-years watching hospital based dramas and has a desperate need to feel included – and off we go through the hospital to the Radiology Department.

Once there Georgina and I were left in a side room. Now here's the thing, because an MRI scan had been ordered, my handcuffs had been removed – an MRI scanner contains extremely powerful electromagnets, so powerful nothing metal including the pins in my chest or the keys and handcuffs on Georgina's belt or the zip on her jacket, are allowed in the room with the scanner. But I'm not going to have an MRI now, I'm having a CT, scan; and then another nurse comes in, and as a matter of routine, checked one last time, that neither I or Georgina had anything metal on us, and gets a nervous reply from Georgina concerning my welfare, should I be behaving this scan at all? The nurse offers reassurance, and then sees the changes made on the notes, MRI scratch CT – perhaps she'd better go double-check with the Radiologist. I imagine phone calls were made and conversations had, the trouble is, it takes nurses ages to answer a ringing phone and all I needed was one minute – well three to be exact. Georgina had her back to me, arms crossed nervously sucking on her teeth. I had a sleeveless medical gown that fastened at the back with two stitched cotton ties, and a pillow. I wound the gown around my hands, looped it around Georgina's neck, put my feet to the small of her back and pulled. To be fair, Georgina didn't give up without a fight, that girl struggled but there comes a point when you're fighting for air, and that's all you're doing, fighting for air, there's no thinking, it's just reaction, and that blind panic just speeds up the inevitable and makes the process of being throttled so much easier – but that's just my theory, you may have your own.

I removed Georgina's shoes and slipped them on; slightly too large but nothing I couldn't manage, and then, clutching the pillow to my chest I stepped out of the side room across a small corridor and into another side room. Inside was an unlocked metal clothes locker containing a pile of men's folded clothes; a pair of brown trousers, a greying white shirt and a drab brown M&S pullover, old man's clothes. All were far too big for my diminutive form and smelt strongly of stale tobacco, but one must be grateful for small mercies. I claimed the pullover, stuffed the pillow down its front and waddled out into the waiting room. Six people sat there, heads buried in magazines or counting the ceiling tiles; only one, a middle-aged woman with a severe fringe and bottle-bottom specs bothered to look up, and she just rolled her eyes at my appearance and returned to her mag. I walked out into the corridor, saw a multitude of signs, none of which said, 'Main Exit;' so followed the one's saying 'Outpatients,' and that's when I saw two security guards heading towards me. They weren't running or alarmed, so I decided to bluff it out and kept going. We were four yards apart when the guard's walky-talky squawked and my nerve broke. I nearly bolted but a door opened in front of me and a nurse appeared carrying an arm full of files, I caught the door behind her and slipped in. It was ward, split by a corridor, with a dorm on either side, each containing six bed spaces. I slipped into the first cubicle and drew the curtain. The bed contained a withered old man with a large medical dressing taped to his bald head. I went straight to his bedside table and found a plastic carrier bag containing faded jogging bottoms, a mismatched tracksuit top, and a pair of truly ancient Puma sneakers were way too big for me, and a wallet containing a single ten-pound note. I dumped the pillow on the bed and stripped to my birthday suit. The old man gave me a good look over and declared, "Star Jumps! Ten Star Jumps!" I obliged, put on his jacket, attempted to touch my toes – a foolhardy thing to do, that sent my spasms through my chest. The old man nodded knowingly and gravely pronounced, "warm up first, always warm up first," and of course he was right. I pulled on the joggers and removed the tenner from the wallet and wafted it in the air, he grinned gave me a thumbs up, proclaiming "go for gold!"

So I gave him another flash of my tits – and our business was concluded.

I was twenty yards from the hospital, heading into the city when I heard the police siren, behind me, I put my head down and kept going, willing my feet not to run. I'd never been to Nottingham before – in that world or my own – so I had no idea where the train station is in relation to the hospital – turns out its just over a mile, and that's no mean feat after six weeks in bed, but I did it. But when I reached the train station and was checking the London timetables, it suddenly occurred to me that all I was doing by getting on a train was giving the authorities a three-hour window to get their shit together. But what other options did I have? – I no longer had a physical ledger to work with, but I maintain that following the precepts and practise of listing, is a healthy mental exercise, and should be encouraged,

OPTIONS	CONS
Steal a car – drive home.	Lousy driver – bound to get myself arrested / killed.
Kidnap driver – steal a car – drive home.	What if they're; A) a lousy driver and get me arrested / killed? B) a hero type driver and get me killed?

	C) have Country & Western music in the car and need to die – killing us both?
Hitchhike home with a trucker.	Violence, risk of rape + + Chocolate?

I walked out of the station and sat on a bench, drained to my very core. My chest ached, and every breath felt like it was wrapped in a lead weight; I figured I'd probably torn some stitches. I began to wonder if being caught might not be such a bad thing and settled down to wait for the boys in blue to catch up. And then I heard a frightened squeal behind me and turned to see two knuckle-draggers in bother-boots giving a redhead teen in a mock-up army camouflage jacket a hard time; I watched impassively, I really didn't have the energy, and then there were pamphlets falling through the air and the knuckle-mutts were pawing the redhead's arse, trying to grab her crotch; that did it. I lifted myself from the bench and stepped into the fray unobserved.

"Oi, dog breath..." Mutt One turned, a sneer fixed to his face, which I broke with my fist. Ordinarily, the blow would have put him into the middle of next week, but I was slow, stiff, and out of shape; and his forehead was made of concrete with very little within it. He staggered back a step or two but came back swinging. Not a problem; I ducked under and put a jab in his side sending him tottering backwards. Meanwhile, his buddy, Mutt Two, saw an opening and took his chance, and planted a boot into my thigh and then tried to repeat the trick; this was a mistake – I caught his foot, tucked it under my arm, and delivered a kick to his crotch of such magnitude, that it's probably closed that gene pool cul-de-sac for good. But it cost me, my chest was immediately engulfed in flame, so that I had to stop and take a breath, and that gave Mutt One time to close in and catch me with a smack on the side of the head that showed me the stars on the other side of the galaxy. I went down, and curled into a ball, expecting the bother boots to come raining in – but a cry went up and four guys in camouflage came charging in; and the next thing I know I'm sitting on a 'Battle Bus:' being offered a hot cup of tea.

"Maybe we should get her to the hospital?" I heard someone say.

"No! I'm good," I insisted.

"You took a n-n-nasty punch to the head," a Jesus lookalike with a stammer informed me.

“She could have concussion,” a taller Jesus lookalike observed, “do you know where you are? Do you know your name? What is her name?”

“I’m fine. I’ve had worse believe me. And my names... Georgina,” I had to come up with something.

“Thank you, Georgina, I don’t know what would have happened if you hadn’t intervened,” the redhead smiled and placed a hand on my shoulder, she had the loveliest greenest eyes I’d ever seen, “really thank you. You were very brave.”

“You shouldn’t have been out there alone Denise?” Yet another Jesus lookalike asserted.

“Don’t tell me that; tell Robbie! where were you Robbie?”

“Yeah, w-w-w-where w-w-w-were you Robbie?” stammering Jesus demanded.

“I needed the toilet. I didn’t ask her to approach those sinners,” Robbie Jesus sulked.

“I didn’t approach them; they grabbed at me. They were like octopuses. It was horrible, I don’t know what would have happened if our friend here hadn’t came along.”

"Yeah, you said," Robbie Jesus grumbled, "you must have provoked them, tempted them."

"I did not!" Denise protested and inadvertently stamped on my foot – I yelped, she buckled, "I'm sorry, I'm so sorry."

"Let us pray," one of the many Jesuses announced, "dear Judith, we thank you for..."

Judith? Who the fuck is Judith? Once the praying and giving of thanks was done, and there was an excess of it, Denise turned her attentions to me, "if you don't want to go to hospital, can we take you home? This is our Battle Bus; we can take you anywhere," this was said with a great deal of pride, "I think we owe you that much."

And I thought, why not try the truth, or at least some of it - so I looked into her beautiful big eyes and said, "I really don't have anywhere to go. I'm pretty much out on a limb here."

Denise smiled, "praise Judith; we can offer you a bed and a place to stay. Have you heard about the love of Judith?"

I couldn't say I had, but I most certainly did.

8

As the Battle Bus - it was an aging London Transport double-decker from some time before comfort – chugged merrily through Nottinghamshire's villages, the wannabe Jesuses; six lads, five lasses (that's how they speak in Nottingham), sang songs of thanks, love and praise to Judith – Judith? Ordinarily, such outrageous behaviour would have exacted a heavy toll from me but given the circumstances, I decided to play along and not indulge in a blood bath. And besides, there was something about Denise and her green-green eyes that rather took my fancy. She had a disarming openness and warmth, that was so unguarded and genuine, that I felt myself drawn into its warmth every time she flashed those green eyes at me; and she was flashing me like a taillight. If you've ever seen a jelly fresh out of its mould and wanted to squeeze it between your fingers, until it was nothing but pulp, then you know what I mean (and should probably seek professional help).

It was dark when we finally arrived back at Temple Hearth, or 'the command centre,' as the Action Man Jesuses referred to it. The place certainly had a presence that was difficult to ignore. It fell somewhere between a Hammer Horror film set and the old house in that black and white version of 'Great Expectations,' – the one in which Alec

Guinness, portrays the world's most irritating flatmate. The house itself smelt strongly of sage and old dogs, of which there seemed to be a boundless supply. We were greeted at the door by the hounds, set about sniffing everybody's crotch in that disconcerting way that dogs do, until they were called off and sent in, by a square shouldered woman with breasts the size of sandbags, and an unruly mop of blue hair that shown like a gas flame; "come in you weary travellers, God bless you all, praise be to Judith for keeping you safe and returning you to our fold, praise be! And who do we have here?"

An account of my intervention and 'rescue' was energetically portrayed – with slight embellishments that did me no harm – and suddenly I was being embraced to an ample bosom that smelt of sweat and Lily of the Valley soap, and hailed as; "a warrior woman, in the spirit of Jael," I was then escorted by Denise and two other rustic blondes to a dormitory on what they referred to as 'the Women's Floor,' and given a brief but succinct guided tour. The eggshell blue communal bathroom contained two showers, a bath and two toilet stalls. A long communal bedroom, divided up with elaborately coloured throws and lacy voiles to accommodate the four (single) female occupants. This led onto a female only 'Meeting Room,' and a small guest room, which had been allotted to me for the night. I was much relieved to discover it had its own bathroom and toilet. It certainly wasn't the Dorchester; the D.I.Y bodge-it plumbing was barely Holiday Inn standards; but it was certainly a step-up from Rampton. I thanked them, slumped down on the bed, and kicked off my acquired shoes, and that's when the weirdness began.

A young woman with a dark complexion, Spanish or perhaps Greek, arrived, carrying a blue plastic washing-up bowl and a bunch of towels – I was about to thank her when she broke into song; her three compatriots instantly harmonised and before I could say "what the fuck Mary Poppins?" Denise was kneeling beside the bed, and my feet were being washed. I immediately stiffened – not as much as Slightly – but she noticed, "are you ticklish? Don't worry, I'll be gentle."

And then the two blondes, their names were Aimee and Lisa, I never worked out which was which, started removing my tracksuit top. I clutched at it and pushed their hands away, but they just started singing in-the-round, as the olive-skinned woman, Beatrice, started combing my hair. It's very difficult to be defensive when someone is brushing your hair, and before I knew it, my tracksuit top was removed, and I was sitting there bare breasted and battered for all to see.

"Oh you poor thing," Aimee or Lisa observed.

"Oh gosh, that looks painful, we'd better call Stella," Denise announced.

And two minutes later, the bosom with the blue hair marched into the room, rubbing her hands together energetically saying, "well let's have a look at you then?" And proceeded to do so, "my dear girl, have you had open heart surgery or something?"

"I was in a car crash. Broke my sternum, crushed my chest," that was more truth than lie.

Stella took me by the shoulder and slowly turned me around. The accompanying chorus of winces was somewhat unsettling. I'd not seen my own reflection since the Susie incident and had no idea what the overall damage looked like, "you've certainly pulled at a couple of sutures there, but nothings actually popped," Stella stated flatly, her hand transferred to my head, "you had all this going on, and you still came to Denise's rescue, you truly are a warrior with Jael's courage. Lord, hear our prayer..." And off they went into fervent prayer for healing and strength, which quickly diverged into an incoherent group-babble that sounded like a mix of Welsh and Muppet faux Dutch. What happened next, I could explain away as fatigue and stress, but to be frank – and who wouldn't want to be Frank? – I really don't understand what happened next; it felt like a flame, rose out of my chest, its heat stifling my lungs, so that I couldn't breathe. I was immediately gripped by a lava spout of panic that I knew would consume me, an orgasm of pain. I was going to burst, die, ripped apart by an emotion I could not name. I cried; I wept till my body shook and my chest was numb and hollow, and then I was hugged – and nobody got hurt. My orgasm of pain was spent. I felt lighter, warm and content – it was terrifying.

I was carried into the shower, and very efficiently washed by many soapy hands, whilst songs of praise and prayers continued – having your minge washed to the sound of 'praise the Lord,' is disconcerting to say the least – and when I emerged, hot, red skinned and smelling of Imperial Leather, the hair brushing and pampering recommenced, and it probably went on after I fell asleep to the sound of the singing 'Sisters of Judith.'

I awoke to song. The room, being brighter, seemed larger and a lot more pleasant than on the night before. There was no clock in the room but it felt early, and when I looked out the window I could see the sun was still low and the expanse of lawn under my window was still covered with a thin blanket of mist, but beyond it, behind a low line of box hedging, there were twenty of so blue clad figures toiling in the garden – and they were singing.

A pile of blue overalls had been left at the end of my bed along with a hideous pair of backless brushed blue velvet slippers, and a disturbingly grey pair of knickers – I gave then a quick sniff; they were clean, so I put them on and got dressed. I should mention here that there was no bra. I don't think anybody there – including the men – wore bras, pendulous Stella certainly didn't.

As I reached the top of the stairs, I could see a mass of circulating dogs below me in the lobby, who alerted by my presence, and being good judges of character immediately started to bark.

"Be quiet you lot, be still, be still!" Stella demanded, as she emerged from the shadows below, and greeted me with an ostentatious salute, "morning sleepy head, come on down, don't mind them, you're a new face that's all. Did we wake you?"

"It's okay, I don't mind... I actually slept really well," I observed with some surprise.

"I'm glad. We're used to early starts here at Temple Hearth, are you hungry? You must be hungry, lets get you something to eat and then I'll get one of the girls to show you around."

Stella grabbed me by the hand and set off down a poorly lit, narrow corridor. I heard the kitchen before I saw it. The sound of harmonising voices was rolling down the corridor towards us, at first, I thought it was the radio and then as we stepped through the door I saw the truth of it; the kitchen was filled with song. It was an extremely old kitchen with a high vented ceiling, butler sinks, and a long wooden table at its centre. Beside the table stood two older women, all dressed in blue, energetically kneading dough, whilst two equally aged men – Moses lookalikes - with balding pates, sat at the other end of the table peeling vegetables; and they were all singing, locked into a complicated overlapping round.

"This is our new disciple, Georgina! The Brave!" Stella sang out in a pitch perfect blast.

"Welcome," the four harmonised, and then went back to their round.

And I'm thinking, "disciple?"

I watched as Stella joined in the round, took a large white loaf, held it under her massive left breast and with a bone handled breadknife, liberally buttered the end of the loaf, and then cut off a doorstop wedge which she then tossed onto my plate. She repeated this display of dexterity and then pushed a large jar of homemade raspberry jam down the

table to me, followed by a skiting tablespoon, accompanied by a floating libretto of, “we give thanks Lord, bless this food, go on, get stuck in, it’s all homemade, in the name of the Lord!”
I tasted, and the jam was good.

Just as I was finishing my last mouthful a series of bells rang out somewhere deep in the old house; and the singing abruptly stopped and the two old girls in the kitchen seemed to plug back into a conversation they’d left undone without a moment’s hesitation, whilst the two old boys immediately broke into peals of laughter that had them doubled up over their pans of vegetables.

“Don’t worry about them dear, it’s just the joy of Judith moving them, it’s their reward for serving our community, the Lord is good,” Stella smiled broadly, as the two old girls started to giggle infectiously, “and its catching, come on, lets see if we can buddy you up.”

I followed Stella’s ample behind out of the kitchen and down another poorly lit corridor that smelt so strongly of sage, my eyes began to water.

“Does the sage bother you?” Stella asked, seeing me wince, “we use it to clear out the negative spirits that our sorties into the outside world are bound to attract. Do you feel the weight of the darkness upon you dear? I think you do, but don't fear, now that you've given yourself to Judith, they can't harm you."

And I'm thinking; "given myself?" But I said, "who is this Judith?"

Stella locked at me quizzically, her gas jet blue hair dancing on top of her head, "I don't understand dear, surely you know the truth of Judith? Denise must have explained who Judith is, I was told you'd accepted her into your heart?"

"Of course... what I meant was, who is she to you?"

Stella quizzical look softened and then broke, "she is my everything. She's the born redeemer, daughter of Christ, the Son of God. And we are called to be her children."

"Amen," it seemed the appropriate response.

"Amen, indeed, and I'm forgetting you that you responded to her call with righteous action. You are blessed my child, and we must do what we can to further your education. Fear not, continue to follow Judith and she will give herself to you," Stella's hand was in my hair, the tips of her fingers tenderly tracing the shape of my earlobe, "I think you'll be able to teach us a thing or two before too long... it's all about being receptive."

“Amen to that,” I responded - why mess with a classic?

I followed Stella through a set of double doors, through a sea of bouncing dogs with crotch magnets fixed to their noses and found myself at the base of the lawn I’d seen from my bedroom, “Denise! Denise! Attend me! Attend me!” Stella sang out in an operatic blast that had the birds flying from the trees. And moments later I heard a fainter but still clear replay of, “I attend, I attend!” and saw Denise jogging across the lawn towards us.

“Bless you Denise,” Stella proclaimed, with a gentle tap to Denise’s nose, “bless you, now Denise, I want you to shepherd Georgina here. It’s only right. The Lord brought her to you, and you deserve the honour, you’ve earnt it.”

“Thank you, Stella,” Denise seemed to shine at the news, “praise Judith, I will do my best.”

“I know it, Denise, I know it. Now then Georgina, young Stella is going to show you around, introduce you to everybody and our ways. Because our ways are not those of the world, ours is the kind path.”

“Amen,” Denise beamed.

Stella pulled us both into her bosom, so that we were nose to nose, immersed in her breasts, as she sang out in full voice, “everybody is here for a reason, and that reason is Judith, Judith has called us to be her children. She called you two, to be, sisters, sisters of power, I know this to be true.”

“Amen,” tears were whelming in Denise’s eyes as she took my hand and squeezed.

What else could I do with an ear full of tit but squeeze back and grin, “Amen.”

We were released and Stella danced back into the house warbling at full volume, yapping dogs in toe.

“Isn’t she wonderful, we’re so blessed,” Denise sighed, still holding my hand.

“Yeah... she’s really something.”

“Isn’t she though. Come on let me show you around,” Denise then began to skip back into the house – I don’t skip, not since I was five – my well-anchored torpor nearly pulled her off her feet, “is something wrong?”

“I don’t skip.”

Denise looked at me vacantly as if I was talking in code and then flushed, so it was almost as red as her hair, “oh my, I’m so sorry, your chest! Of course you can’t skip, I’m so sorry. You just get so used to it here, we’re always singing and skipping everywhere...”

“Why?”

“Our Lord taught Judith to skip and to sing and foretold that her laugh will heal the world, we follow in her path, we are called to be her children.”

“Singing, skipping and laughing.”

“As children for the Lord.”

“Sounds exhausting,” – I meant irritating.

“It can be, that’s why we need God’s love and the strength of our brothers and sisters to help us along the path.”

I gave Denise my cheesiest grin – smiling supresses the gag reflex.

Denise proceeded to show me around the homestead, the effort it took her to suppress her need to skip along like a blissed-out wallaby, was gratifying and yet oddly grating, sometimes she hoped ahead declaring, “and this is the chapel, I love the chapel, Stella lives above the chapel so she can be near prayer all day long, isn’t that beautiful!” And then she’d shuffle in place as if she were desperate to pee, “we can’t go in now because its midmorning prayers. We have morning prayers, midmorning prayers, midday prayers and Evensong, but most of the day is caught up with singing and praying anyway and as Stella says it doesn’t matter where you pray, as long as you pray. Judith’s song was heard throughout the land! And that’s the Repenting Room; I don’t like the...”

"Denise!" I had to interrupt her babble with a pinch to the nipple – no bra.

"Ow! Why'd you do that?"

"To get you attention... I feel like I'm missing something here. I stepped into help you out last night, and you guys gave me a lift back... which was nice... but now, I seem to be a disciple. I'm told I've accepted someone called Judith into my life, and the funny thing is... I don't remember doing it. What's going on?"

Denise looked bashfully into her own brushed blue slippers, and blushed, "don't you remember?"

"Don't bullshit me Denise, you'll regret it."

Denise slumped down onto the floor and put her head in her hands, "oh sweet Judith, what have I done?"

"That's what I'm asking Denise, what have you done?"

"I told everybody you heard the song of Judith telling you to intervene at the train station, and that you gave your life to her on the bus."

"Why?"

"I don't know. I got carried away, it was such an awful night, Robbie was being horrible to me, and nobody else wanted to handout the leaflets, and then those boys started grabbing me, and then you turned up, and I ... we are called to be her children! I knew Judith had called you to save me. So I told myself you'd accepted Judith as your mistress and saviour, and... I just wanted to please Stella."

"That's ..." I was lost for words, "that's... so dumb."

"I'm such a sinner," Denise blubbed.

"I'm not sure what that means, but it's certainly not good is it Denise? It's like extreme needy, needy to the max. Not good Denise."

"I know. I'm in so much trouble," she buried her head in hands and whimpered like a scalded dog.

Memories of our dog, Wiggy, running around our kitchen in terrified pain flooded back, and that awful remembrance of a emotions you could drown in, and there was only one way I knew to deal with such a pain – block it; "fuck it, I don't care. As long I know what's going on I don't mind, but you've got to understand, I'm not hanging around, as soon as I can, I'm gone."

Denise jumped to her feet, "okay, that's fine."

"And you really ought to know, I'm not nice Denise, I'm really not nice."

Denise's propensity for blushing must have been genetic because she boiled up a beauty that time, "I think you're lovely, and maybe you'll want to stay once you get to know us? Once you feel the love of Judith, I know you'll want to stay."

"And I think, once you get to know me, you'll want me to go. You'll probably run away screaming."

Denise giggled and then she popped up onto her toes and danced around in a twirling circle, "it's the Joy of Judith! I feel the Joy of Judith rising in me!"

"Whoopee-do, now listen, I'm telling you now, if you think you can change me, forget it, I'm a hopeless case."

"You're funny," Denise's hand swept down the front of my blue overalls, her finger flicking my nipple – no bra, "there's always hope. Maybe you should get some rest, get your strength back. You might need it later."

She didn't mean what I thought she meant, but she was right. Evensong is called Evensong because it happens on the eve of the next day; not because they have fun entertainments; dancing, chanting and Even Song; how was I supposed to know, I was raised a heathen. As it turned out their Evensong, did have a lot of dancing, chanting and singing. It was a midnight rave without the drugs, alcohol or cool lighting, but the Judiths went at it hard for nearly two hours. I had the honoured position of 'new disciple' but as I was also 'injured in the line of duty,' I was excused the bopping about and was allowed the hallowed spot amongst the abundant scatter cushions. I was however forcibly prayed for several times and had Stella's boobs in my face on multiple occasions.

On the fifth buffeting, she took my hand, bid me rise from my cushions, and led me to the front of the chapel – the chancel, I believe it's called - and stood me there facing the humming congregation, "And now sister Georgina, will bear witness, and tell us of her calling..."

Do what? – I glared at Denise, who winced, shrugged and then blushed.

"Tell us how Judith called you to be her child," Stella graciously elucidated.

Fair enough, I thought, "So, I was just out of...."

"Sing it sister sing it!" I barrage of voices demanded.

"Do what?"

"Use the voice Judith gave you sister, sing," Stella grinned.

I've never had much of a voice, I've never wanted much of a voice, and now I was expected to sing in front of a crowd of strangers – Nightmare Fuuuuck! I didn't even know where to start, and then I recalled Slightly and his Streisand obsession, "...the suns a ball of butter, don't bring around a cloud to rain on my parade, I heard her say... fight and fight even harder, smash them in the teeth, hear them shatter, I heard her say, so I fought and I fought even harder, smashed him in the balls, see them scatter, Judith is coming to town today!"

Silence... an awkward long silence, holding your breath, open jawed silence.

"We are called to be her children!" Stella boomed, and a roar of triumph shook the rafters, as the congregation went apeshit! I was pulled so tightly into Stella's chest I couldn't breathe, and instantly felt that locked up volcano cocktail of rage and terror rising from my centre, an orgasmic agony that was going to shatter me and blow me apart – again I saw poor scalded Wiggy running around our kitchen; I couldn't let myself feel that much ever again, I couldn't let it happen, it would kill me! I buried my head deeper into Stella breasts, and wished myself a thousand miles away, lost in space, floating free, gagging on nothingness – and then I heard it, a deep resonant snorting behind me. I turned to see the chapel filled, from floor to rafters, with the massive bulk of the blood moon unicorn. The beast had found me, and knew me as one of its own. The beast's throat rumbled like low thunder. I felt it resonate in my centre as peace, ice cold peace, flowed through me. The chapel was a maelstrom of emotionally charged singing, but I was the chilled ice-cube of serenity wedged between Stella's breasts, and I knew, whatever else was happening, I must ready myself to go, for I have heard the call to return home.

As the proceedings began to wind down, I sat back and watched the groups interactions. There were the young male Judiths, Jesus-lookalikes one and all, and the aging Judiths and their attached Moses-lookalikes, and all the young juicy Judiths, a fine band of young beauties it had to be admitted, and then it struck me – there were no children. Where were the children? There were plenty of married or at least attached couples, but no children. I hadn't seen any children at Temple Hearth for the entire day, and then I saw Stella embracing the young Judiths each in turn, clutching them to her unfettered pillow sized breasts, which they invariably kissed – or was it suckled? What the fuck was going on? I saw her hand lingering here and there, stroking hair, brushing a cheek, blessing a forehead, and then as she pulled Denise into herself and I saw the gentle caress to the cheek, that strayed to the ear – I got it: Stella had a good thing going, and the making of children didn't come into it. No doubt the Beloved Judith was childless, so we were called to be her children, but not to make them. I got it, and I really didn't want to leave. I wanted to be Stella.

9

For the next three days I had Denise at my beck and call, and she was very attentive, but not one beck passed without her passing on some snippet, insight, or appreciation of the 'Beloved Judith.' I have an instinctive aversion to unabashed enthusiasm; be it trainspotting, birdwatching or boy bands; but Denise's immersion in the Beloved Judith, I found fascinating and repugnant – like the lifecycle of a tapeworm. So, no matter how strong the urge to bash in her head became, the need to know what had attracted Denise to her Beloved Judith grew within me: what was in it for her? And then, late in the night of the second day I heard myself say, "how did you get into this Judith stuff?" And as soon as the words had left my mouth, I heard the trap that had been laid for me spring shut; that girl had her witness mechanism oiled, cocked and ready to go.

"My dad left when I was thirteen and I found it really difficult. I'd always been his little girl, and he just went off and started a whole new family without me, it really hurt. And then mum met this guy who she really liked and seemed really nice, he treated me us real well, taking us out and spending money on us. And then they got married and things changed, I used to catch him looking at me, looking me up and down, and then one night he crept into my bedroom and started touching me inappropriately and..."

"Did you kill him?"

"What? No, I didn't kill him."

"Did Judith kill him?"

"No, of course not."

"Do you want him dead? Did you want to kill him?"

"No! I forgave him."

"Right... well that's a great story. Another abuser gets away with it. Nice one Judith."

"Judith died on a wheel for me. She forgave those who put her there, and if she can do that for me, I can forgive Nigel."

"Nigel? And what's this Nigel doing with your forgiveness? Has Nigel turned over a new leaf? Is Nigel feeding peeled grapes to the starving millions in Africa? Or is he still fucking your mum? Or has he moved onto other little girls?" Denise's face froze, but I could see the heat rising behind the eyes. "So, he's still with your mum, so the rest of the story goes like this; you told your mum, but mum didn't believe you, is that it? More than that! Much more than that? I got it, she blamed you; she backed him and blamed you. And then you left, or she threw you out, right?" Denise's jaw had set like a cornerstone, but her eyes were like fire. There was nothing she wanted to do more than claw out my eyes, and it was taking everything she had to resist that urge, the air tingled with energy, "come on Denise, what's stopping you? Forgive me, that's what you do right? Sing a little ditty, give a little dance and pretend it never happened, la la la, all better now."

"Why are you being so mean?"

"Why are there no children here? Why are there no babies?"

"Judith calls us..."

"Yeah, yeah. I get it, Judith calls us to be her children, and children can't have children, I get it, and I like it, it's perfect for me. I hated being a child when I was one, but you, your choosing Judith out of fear, you don't want to pass the poison on, that's why you're here, you don't serve Judith, Judith serves you, and the only thing you want to do is hide."

I could see Denise's thermostat was about to blow by the vapour condensing behind her eyes and I knew, if it blew, it was likely to rip my head off, but I couldn't stop, "I'm sorry D, did I touch on some truth there, come on D, you know what to do, give me some absolution, and pretend it didn't happen."

Denise raised her fist, opened her mouth in a scream, and I grabbed her, pulled her in close, rolled her onto the bed and buried my hands in her hair and my tongue in her mouth.

I'm going to draw a discreet veil over the following proceedings; not because I'm shy but to cause you as much discomfort and frustration as I possibly can; you perve. But I will say this - yes like a train, backwards, forwards, sideways, couldn't see straight and within an inch.

Denise's post-coital guilt descended like a tugboat falling from forty thousand feet, hard and fast.

"Oh my god what have I done?"

"About everything in the book with a couple of notes made in the margin."

"That's not funny!"

“Impressive is what it is, and I’d like to thank you for flying Les-Airways, be sure to come again... if you can manage it.”

“Stop it,” this time the tears came pouring and before I could grab her naked little behind, it was streaking from the room.

I got up and closed the door. I knew they’d be a commotion, but I had no idea what to expect and so... went to sleep, believe me, I was fucked.

I was rudely awakened by Stella and four Jesus lookalikes storming into the room, brandishing bibles and babbling their bonkers faux Welsh like a battle cry. Half asleep and still recovering from an epic clit bashing, I was caught off guard, wrapped up in a bed sheet and carried from the room before I could enjoy the first fart of the day; it was very efficiently done. I was aware of being carried down many flights of stairs before being unceremoniously dumped naked as a babe in a dark room that smelt of damp, mushrooms and old wet paper. I sat there shivering, convinced I could hear rats circling until my eyes finally adapted to the gloom of the room and I could differentiate the doorframe from the wall. Feeling around it, I located the light switch and illuminated the room, in the weak light of a single bare bulb. It was some kind of vegetable cellar, long abandoned and now occupied by nothing but piles of old newspapers bound in twine and a significant community of startled silverfish. I sat on one of the bales and reflected on my situation – and no matter what angle I looked at it from, I reckoned I was pretty-much fucked. Either this was retribution for my night of pleasure or the Judith's had discovered who I really was and had dumped me in their dungeon till the authorities turned up. This seemed less likely but I couldn't rule it out, at least not until the door swung open and six Jesus-looking-Judiths, and Stella marched into the room, formed a circle around me, bibles aloft and proceeded to babble chant over me, at a decibel rate any Heavy Metal band would be proud of; these saps were shredding their throats screaming at me. And I let them, and then I considered what my response was supposed to be, what were they expecting to see? And I gave it to them, I rolled around on the floor, covered myself in dirt, tore at my hair, screamed in pain, crouched down and pissed myself and finally collapsed into a heap; and only then did my ring of tormentors fall silent.

"Judith, sweet Judith save me, save me," I whimpered.

"Amen! Thank you Judith!" replied the chorus.

"Do you repent of your sins?" Stella demanded.

“I do, I do, I’m a sinner, a terrible, terrible sinner, Judith forgive me!”

A chorus of amens filled the small room.

Stella braced herself, spread her legs and lowered her breasts, till they hung like Damocles udders above me, “Repent and believe in God’s one true daughter, Judith the Saviour, the lamb of God!”

“Does that come with mint sauce?” I just couldn’t help myself.

“Sinner!” Stella shouted, nearly toppling over as she swung her bible at my head. I grabbed the book with both hands and rolled under her swaying breasts. This put Stella’s centre of gravity dangerously askew. She tottered forward, lost her balance and came crashing down. Jumping to my feet, I snatched the book from her grasp and smashed it across her face. Nowhere near fatal but guaranteed to induce a headache she’d never forget. Seeing their hero felled triggered the classic range of instinctive responses from the gathered faithful; two froze, two ran for the door, and two stepped forward to save Stella. Unfortunately for them automatic responses are rarely coordinated. One dived over Stella in order to protect her and the other swung at me. This heroic act was hampered by the cramped conditions and the two frozen bystanders; one of which caught my would-be assailants backswing with his nose, whilst the other provided a useful distraction by bolting for the door, tripping over God knows what, and cracking his head against the wall with such force, we all felt the echo in our teeth. This double whammy, distracted my assailant long enough for me to reset my posture, distribute my weight and deliver a kick to his crutch that bounced his balls off the back of his teeth; he went down – and I was running, stark-bollock(less)-naked, out the door and up a flight of stairs.

I emerged into the crowded kitchen, the gathered kitchen Judiths immediately scattered, all but one, Aimee (possibly Lisa); "what have you done?"

"What have I done? I kicked their butts and I'm about to kick yours," I grabbed a knife from the kitchen drawer and advanced on her, backing her into a corner.

"Please don't, I'm sorry, don't hurt me, don't hurt me!"

I heard a stammering cry of, "g-g-get her!" rising from the stairs behind me.

"Is there a key to that door?"

Aimee (?) shook her head, "but there is a deadbolt." She was right, there were two, one at the top, one at the bottom. I slammed the door shut, threw the bolts, and then looked Aimee/Lisa up and down; she was wearing a purple baggy jumper, grubby jeans and ugly brown hiking boots. I fixed her with my best cold stare; "Strip!"

"What?"

"Strip! Give me your clothes, I'm naked and I don't want to be."

The door behind me was being pounded with angry fists and prayers of retribution!

"Oh...okay. You're not going to hurt me are you?"

I raised the knife, "this is not a fucking discussion, give me your clothes!" She started to undress. I took the opportunity to fill the sink with cold water and douse myself down, "where's that bitch Denise?"

"They locked her in the Repenting Room," was the reply.

"They did what?"

"They locked her in the Repenting Room next to the chapel. She confessed to Stella. What did you think would happen? Stella likes to keep the young chicks for herself, and she'll defend her brood."

I couldn't hide my astonishment, "you know about Stella?"

"We've all been in Stella's prayer room, some of us like it... some take more convincing than others, Stella likes those best. She's been working on Denise for a while now. You took her toys away. She's not going to let that go."

I suddenly wished I'd put a brick across the back of Stella's head, "what will she do with Denise?"

Aimee/Lisa shrugged, threw me her jeans and stood there in her grey panties, looking at me disapprovingly with her hands on her hips, "I guess Stella will come up with some kind of penance, I doubt Denise will enjoy it. And then Stella will declare her penance paid, forgive her and kiss it all better."

"Shit... these boots are horrible. How can you bear to wear these things? Go on piss off, get out of here."

"Open this d-d-door! Open this d-d-d-d-door! At once!" the voice shouted, as fists and feet shuddered the door. It was a redundant demand, the screws holding the bolts were fast losing their grip. I had a decision to make, run or be overwhelmed by maddened Judiths – I ran. I ran down the corridors, back into the house, back to the chapel. The 'Repenting Room' was locked with another ancient deadbolt,

I threw it open, expecting the worst – and there was Denise, sitting in an armchair sipping on a mug of herbal tea.

“What are you doing?” I shouted.

“What are you doing?” she shouted back.

“Getting us out of here, come on, we need to go.”

“Go where?”

“Anywhere! Away from here, we need to go!” I could hear the baying of dogs and enraged Judiths barrelling through the corridors, “we need to get out of here now!”

Denise calmly placed her mug on the arm of her chair and announced, “I’m not leaving. I belong here. But you should go.”

“Denise, this isn’t real, this is just another layer of abuse.”

“And would I be any better off with you? You told me you weren’t nice, you weren’t lying. You should go; I’m staying.”

Dumbfounded is the word, utterly dumbfounded. I heard the dogs crashing into the wall of the connecting corridor behind me and fled down the sage stinking corridor and out of the double doors onto the lawn. Running in my newly acquired boots was neither comfortable or easy – they felt like lead weights attached to my feet, but as soon as I heard the doors behind me shatter and the yapping of the excited dogs, I found a well of adrenaline I did not know I had. I cleared the low hedge at the end of the garden and landed in a freshly dug vegetable plot. Twenty yards ahead sat a wooden jetty and a stream – if I could cross it, I'd be beyond the Judith's rage and out of their reach. I turned to see the dogs charging towards the hedge; I wasn't going to make it. There was a garden fork to my left, I grabbed it and did exactly what you think I did to the first dog that cleared the hedge; and the second and the third – the other two bolted and I followed suit, towards the river.

The jetty was rotten, the boards soft to the touch, it started creaking and cracking as soon as I stepped on to it. Shouts of outrage and screams of horror broke out behind me as the Judiths cleared the hedge and found their dogs; three of the Jesus lookalikes were already racing towards me. There was no boat, and probably hadn't been for twenty years, the jetty was an abandoned fixture they were waiting for the river to wash away; and it surely would because that was no small meandering stream, that thing had pace and it looked deep. The other bank was a good eight yards away. I was not a strong swimmer (early morning starts + swimming pool + swimsuit + changing rooms = perverts). I wasn't sure

I could make it, but what option did I have? I faltered for a moment, turned to face my pursuers, and then the jetty interceded and dropped me into the river.

It was cold, bitingly cold, and had more current than I'd bargained for; I rose once, kicking and spitting, and was instantly dragged down and dragged along the bottom of the river like a piece of trash. My right knee collided with something, and the jarring pain had me sucking in water. The pressure on my chest was immense, it felt like I was going to implode, like I was being crushed and then it occurred to me, "you're drowning! And it hurts! Drowning hurts!" And then I broke surface and slammed into the side of something very solid. I felt myself being dragged under and knew I was lost, I was done, I went under. I felt something snag my shoulder and twist me about but I'd already given myself to the water, I was done and the world went out.

When I came to, there was an old man sitting astride me, pumping my chest, but I was too weak to protest.

"There she is, you got her Joe, you got her," I heard a female voice proclaim.

I was turned onto my side and a thick blanket placed over me as I proceeded to throw up a river of my own, between aching gasps for breath.

“Let’s get to shore, she needs to be in hospital,” the male voice panted.

“There’s a phone at the Goat and Barge,” the woman, who I still could not see, announced.

“Sure, or we could try one of these houses along the river, they’ll have a phone, it’s probably quicker.”

“Only if they’re in, we know the Goat and Barge is open, its only fifteen minutes away.”

The old man said no more, and moments later the heavy slow chug of a diesel engine reverberated the wooden deck below me. I rolled onto my back and looked up into a grey blue sky that really wanted to rain; I’d never been so pleased to see clouds. A thin face, with a sharp nose moved into my line of vision. Her eyes were stonewashed blue and her grey hair hung either side of her face in two long plaits, that were tied off in two large bright red bows – it was an incongruous look, that was only highlighted by the broadest, most beautiful smile I’ve ever seen – even if the teeth were a bit yellow.

“Hello there, how you doing? Can you hear me? What’s your name dear? Did you fall off a boat?”

The engine dropped into neutral, and the old man's squarer but none the less handsome face reappeared, "I didn't think of that," I was forcibly sat up, "were you alone? Were there others?" His voice was firm, his eyes wide with alarm.

I tried to answer but I couldn't speak. My throat felt greasy and red raw. I shook my head and clutched at my throbbing knee and watched a red wave run through my fingers.

"Shit, she's bleeding," the old man snapped.

"Let me see," the old lady pushed him aside, and examined the free-flowing gash above my knee, "that's going to need stitches, get me some gauze from the box Joe."

Joe did as he was told and returned with a large red First-Aid box. The old lady busied herself in a very professional manner and soon my leg was tightly bound in gauze bandage, "there you go dear, that will do until we get you to the hospital. What's your name dear?" I clutched at my throat; it would do nothing but rasp. "Don't fret dear, that will be the water, it won't last long. Joe, can we get her inside, she's shivering."

"It's probably shock. Better not move her around too much, just keep her warm till we get to the Goat."

The old lady nodded but I could see she was making her own assessment, “Joe, I want her inside.”

“I can’t steer and carry her!” Joe protested.

“Well, you’re not steering now, so let’s get her inside quick so you can get back to steering.”

“What if she’s a suicide? Did you put yourself in the...” a glare from the old girl stopped his sentence short, and then I was being very gently guided below deck into a snug barge that smelt of diesel, lavender and cough sweets. I was placed on a low bench covered with a sturdy but worn cushion beside a large carpetbag filled with balls of wool and knitting needles. As I was released, I grabbed up the needles and held them to the old man’s throat.

“Jesus! What now?” he protested.

“That’s my knitting!” the old woman protested.

I waved her onto the opposite bench and then pulled the old man down beside me, keeping the needles tight to his throat. Again, I tried to speak, but it was useless, I gritted my teeth and glared at the old woman, willing her to understand me – and the oddest thing happened.

“You don’t want to go the hospital... very well but...” she wagged a bony finger at my leg, “you really should you know, you nearly drowned, you probably need shots, there's all sorts in the rivers, there's tetanus..."

"Weill's disease," the old man offered.

"Cryptosporidium, that will make you shit through the eye of a needle that one. And you've had water in your lungs, that could your compromise your respiratory system you're young, but you could still go into cardiac arrest."

There was something about the old woman's ability to list possible damnations that I found incredibly appealing; she was a sister in the negative ledger. I felt something in my throat and gagging coughed up a chunk of green goo, the old man made to pull away and was about to throw a punch, I couldn't have avoided, when we heard voices shouting from the riverbank.

"Hello, hello there, have you seen a young w-w-woman in the river, she f-f-fell off our jetty, and we can't f-f-find her."

Joe's eyes narrowed, "Which jetty was that then?"

"Temple Hearth, about a quarter of a mile d-d-downstream, the big white house on the right bank."

Joe released my wrists, "no we've not seen nothing," and then pushed my hands away, as he stepped up onto the deck, "it's more likely she crossed to the other side, if she could swim, could she swim?"

Noises and affirmations of thanks were made, and then Joe reappeared, "Judiths ... were you escaping that lot?" I nodded. "Put the needles down pet, you won't need them. Maggie, get the lass a hot drink, we'll take her wherever she wants to go."

"She should go to hospital," Maggie insisted.

"Well, I don't reckon that's happening Maggie, let's get down river, and get some distance between us and them bastards."

Maggie's scowl was fierce but not unkind, like a strict elementary teacher, "You've ruined my shawl. I've been working on that for two days. My needles if you please dear."

I handed over the knitting needles and rasped "Sorry," though it cost me dear.

"Not to worry, nothing I can't do again. Let's find you some dry things. I've got nothing but old lady clothes I'm afraid.... but I think I've got you some old boots that are better than those..."

And at those words I fell in love with Maggie and passed out.

10

Although I escaped cryptosporidium, tetanus and Weill's disease, I did run a fever for several days. Battered, bruised and weakened with fever, I felt hot and yet felt none too hot, as we say in England – ill is what I was. And boy did I dream, mad stuff, way beyond blood unicorns, way beyond stone carvings that eat old ladies – this was delirium shit, exploding cats, flesh eating wasps, talking cornflakes with opinions on the prison system, and torch carrying claustrophobic Tampax – really weird stuff.

The boat was called 'The Abigail,' although the inside did resemble a paisley psychedelic fever dream, the outside was decorated in the traditional fashion, primary-coloured panels framed in gold over a tar black background. Maggie had covered the deck with a zoo's worth of knitted animals, baby clothes and shawls which she either sold at locks and marinas or gifted to children walking along the towpaths. Although Maggie swathed me in knitted blankets, I did manage a few hours stretched out on the narrowboats roof, laying amongst the woollen zoo, watching the world pass at duck speed. It was not entirely unpleasant experience. And I believe, I did feel relaxed or awhile there, relaxed and oddly at ease with myself – it was a diamond moment but unlike diamonds, not made to last.

The next day I was back on the deck, huddled amongst the knitted menagerie, with a throat too tender to tolerate communication. Maggie supplied me with a pen, so I could scrawl notes when I required assistance or, as she said, "had the urge to converse."

'Where we going?' Was an early question. To which Joe replied, "just following the river, heading south. We're on the Trent heading into Lincolnshire, where we'll met up with the Witham... go with the flow."

I scrawled another note and handed it to him, it read, "I need to get down south, as near to Basingstoke as possible."

Joe read the note, reached into a draw and unfolded a huge, waxed map, which he studied intently for several minutes; "yeah we can do that, it's going to take the best part of a week, but we've nothing better to do. Unless you want us do drop you off at a bus stop or a train station?" I shook my head. "In that case, sit back and chill out ... let's go with the flow ... go with the flow," Joe intoned the words as if they were a mantra, "go with the flow."

"Go with the flow," Maggie chimed in from the cabin.

I was instantly opposed to the very idea of travelling by boat; bother Ratty and Mole! How could anyone tolerate such a lackadaisical approach to getting from A to B? Where were the plans, the itinerary, the timetables? Luckily my irritation was quickly soothed by Joe's recitation of the rules of the waterways, local bylaws and expected forms of behaviour at mariners, locks and private moorings. Boating may look easy-going and laidback, but it's about as relaxed as a constipated ferret – and I found this very reassuring – imagine having nothing to kick against; my mind would melt.

I felt better the next morning, despite finding myself clad in a pink woolly sweater, a matching bobble hat, and scarf - whilst being spoon fed tinned chicken noodle soup, by an old lady I'd threatened to kill with a knitting needle only a few days before – something had to be said.

"I'm really sorry about the whole knitting needle thing Maggie," I manged to whisper, my throat still felt like it was lined with razor blades.

"Gone and forgotten dear, you were scared that's all. We all were. Those Judiths are enough to put the wind up anyone."

"You know the Judiths?"

"Yes. Not those ones. Believe me, you're best out of it love."

The engine stopped its throbbing and a few minutes later Joe appeared, wiping the sweat from his brow with a grease-stained rag, "and how's our invalid doing?"

"Better," I rasped.

"That throat still sounds sore," Joe winced.

"Hardly surprising," Maggie asserted, "that's what happens when you drink polluted water. Suzy..." – that being the name I offered them – "was asking about the Judiths."

"Was she?" Joe placed a hand on Maggie's head and gently stroked it, but his eyes met mine and they were firm and inquisitive, "when did you fall in with them?"

I quickly scribbled out my answer and handed it to Joe, "A few days ago, at a train station. I was just out of hospital and had nowhere to go. They offered me a place to stay."

Joe nodded and sighed as he looked to Maggie, "yeah, that's their M.O. Pick off the low hanging fruit."

"Joe!" Maggie glared.

Joe shrugged, "no offence intended. We were low hanging fruit ourselves once, bloody windfalls we were," Joe proceeded to kick off his boots, revealing thick pink woollen socks, with a hole worn through by the big toe on each foot, "and this little piggy went to market," he chuckled somewhat woefully. "Our daughter, Abigail, joined the Judiths ten years ago, she was fourteen..."

"Nearly fifteen," Maggie asserted.

"Nearly fifteen, we didn't think much about it at first. Kids have these religious phases, best not to make too much of it we thought. Then at sixteen she moves into one of their Temples, not the one you saw, this was down in Dorset. We didn't like it, but again we didn't want to make too much of it, she seemed happy enough, and then two years later the police come calling..." Joe suddenly withdrew into himself, visibly withering beside me on the bench.

"Abigail accused Joe of molesting her," Maggie stated.

"Rape is what she accused me of... sexual abuse and rape."

"There wasn't a word of truth in it," Maggie was a rock and would countenance no contradiction.

"Try telling that to the world. I was arrested and charged. But two years later, a week before the case was due in court, all charges were dropped. No case to answer... which somehow, isn't the same as being found innocent."

They both fell into their own private silences, neither connecting with the other, each consumed by their own pain, until Maggie lifted her head and addressed the boats painted ceiling, "about a year later we received a letter from Abigail asking us to forgive her. She still considered herself a believer but said she wanted to come home," she choked on the words. Joe's hand found Maggie's knee; she grasped it with both hands like a lifeline. "We told her to come home. But we never saw her again. She took her own life. The Judiths were to blame. They talked her into testifying against me and then rejected her... such a terrible, terrible waste."

"We made the mistake of trying to take on the Judiths, holding them to account. You don't cross an organisation like that and get away with it. Friends in high places. Whatever we had left we lost."

"Don't mess with the Judiths," Maggie's voice cracked, "we lost everything, our good name, our business, our house."

I considered the old man in the dirty overalls sitting beside me; he didn't look like an abuser. But they seldom did, at least not until they were caught. I could see that something dark laid across Joe's shoulders but lacked the ability to discern its hue; was that guilt, shame or loss? Whichever it was, it was making me feel uncomfortable, I had to suggest a solution, "do you want them dead? We could go back and slaughter the lot of them?"

Maggie's face was stricken, "and then what?"

"And then... other stuff will happen, but they'd be dead."

"No, we don't want them dead," Maggie insisted.

"I did want them dead," Joe sighed, "but not anymore," Joe must have seen the look of bafflement on my face, "I want them to acknowledge the damage they've done, I want them to acknowledge and live with what they've done, and above all else, make sure it never happens to anyone else."

I thought, "Good luck with that, you want hypocrites who forgive themselves for all their wrongdoings to admit to their crimes," but wrote – "Not going to happen."

"Probably not, but that's what I want. I want them to be human. I have to believe they're human."

I couldn't comprehend Joe's thinking then and I'm not sure I fully grasp it now – I certainly can't see it catching on.

Late that night, long after we'd all retired to our allotted zones; me on the bench/bed and them in their cabin, I lay there looking up at that painted ceiling, tracking the path of the paisley vines and counting the tiny birds, trying not to work myself up into a lather; it didn't work. I just couldn't see how good folks like Joe and Maggie expected to survive in the world with such attitudes? Who chooses to be a sheep in a world of wolves? It was irresponsible, it was fairytale nonsense that left you harbouring a convicted murderer in your narrowboat ... and feeding them chicken noddle soup. It was madness, and yet, that madness had saved my life.

We travelled like that for a couple of days; Joe steering the boat, and Maggie knitting or opening tins of soup, and the all the time, the two of them chatting away with all the energy of two people who have just bumped into each other after years apart. I can't remember for the life of me what they talked about, but it was always warm and gentle, I don't think I'd ever heard two people talk so much, and say so little; and not wanted to cave their heads in. Normally such adorable behaviour would have me seething or retching but these two old farts had me completely entranced – I must have been very ill.

A few days later I was trying to make myself more useful and was giving Joe a hand as we passed through a flight of staircase locks. A process that is both archaic and laborious but not without its charms. It entails the isolation of a chamber of water, which is then lowered or raised to connect with another isolated chamber. This process is repeated until the height of the water carrying the barge matches that of a new stretch of water, enabling vessels to move up and downhill, from one waterway to another. I was standing on the canal path beside Joe, whilst Maggie minded the wheel, when I heard voices raised in song. I looked up to see a group of figures dressed in army fatigues crowded around an ice-cream van parked in a layby a short distance from the canal, behind which loomed a bloody great London bus. I immediately deserted Joe and jumped back onto the boat and hid myself below deck. Joe must have worked it out for himself, and I heard him say; "keep your eyes on the bow Maggie. Go with the flow."

I was still crouched below deck as we passed through the fourth and final lock, when I heard a familiar male voice call out, "hello there, w-w-w weren't you up the Trent earlier in the week?"

"Yes, that's right," Joe replied stiffly.

"W-w-we met. W-w-were looking for a f-f-friend who f-f-fell in the river?"

"That's right, so you were. I remember. Did you find her?"

"Oh yeah, she's f-f-fine. No harm d-d-done."

"Glad to hear it. Well, that's a relief, I am pleased."

"Glad to bring g-g-good tidings. Where you heading?"

"Nowhere special, just going with the flow, take care now."

"Love the name of your boat. Have a safe journey Abigail, and all that sail on her."

Joes voice dropped into a low growl, "and fuck you too."

The engine revved, the water rippled and we were chugging on our way. Moments later Maggie stepped down into the cabin, clutching three coffee mugs, a look of consternation fixed to her face.

"He saw the mugs. I saw him counting them. And now he can identify us."

It went without saying that the Judith's would have Joe and Maggie's names on file. They'd be listed as enemies, persecutors, just the kind of unbelievers to give succour to a dangerous element such as myself. Someone the Judiths must have discovered by now, was an escaped felon, and a homicidal lunatic. I realised I was one phone call away from capture. You can't outrun the police on a narrowboat.

"There's something you should know..." I informed Maggie, "and it's not nice."

That night we moored Abigail beneath a vast overhanging willow on the canals offside, far from the commonplace moorings. It would have been poor cover by day and wouldn't present much of a challenge to a patrol boat with a searchlight, but it was much less accessible, and the draping foliage provided a reassuring, if illusory sense of safety.

Maggie and Joe had taken the news that they were harbouring a mass murderer better than I had any right to expect. At first, they doubted the validity of my story. I suspect it was easier to consider the whole thing delusionary, the product of poisoned water and fever. At worst I was a mentally ill person that required care not condemnation – 'I hadn't done them any harm' they protested, until I reminded them of the knitting needle incident. But they persisted in their good opinion, preferring to see me as the victim of a shared enemy and an ally in their cause, someone worth saving, other than what I really was, a very real threat to their own safety – they really weren't very bright. And then we sat down together around the cabin's collapsable table, listening to a BBC Radio 4 News broadcast, updating the nation on the ongoing search for my vile self. Say what you like about the BBC, but they certainly know how to clarify a situation.

"Police continue to search for the escaped mass murderer Anna Codner, who escaped from a hospital in..."

"That's not your name," Maggie insisted, "that's not you."

"No, that is me. My real name is Anna, not Suzy."

Maggie deflated, "I find this very difficult to believe, I'm sure it can't be as bad as all that."

"Codner was detained under the Mental Health act after a series of brutal attacks in her hometown of Basingstoke, in which five people were murdered..." the newsreader went on to list my deeds, my subsequent detention and the official advise to, "do not approach but report all sighting to the official hotline or call 999..."

"Did you do what they're saying you did?" Joe rasped.

"Sure did... and worse, if I'm being honest."

“Suzy... how could you?” Maggie sniffed – I’d never felt such shame.

I’d been a hairsbreadth away from believing that Maggie, Joe and I could be a family unit. A fresh start in a happy family from a simpler time. I really think I wanted it to be true. Even if I knew it couldn’t be, because it wasn’t my world, I wasn’t of their world – I was adrift on a doppelgänger world, a fugitive in another reality. I had encroached into the peace and tranquillity of two good people’s lives, and I sensed, if I stayed, Joe and Maggie’s peaceful oasis would end up being trampled underfoot, and I couldn’t let that happen.

“I want to thank you both for everything you’ve done for me. I’ve really enjoyed our time together, and I wish we could have more, but I don’t want to bring any more trouble down on you. You’re lovely people and you deserve better. So, here’s what we’re going to do...”

After tying Joe and Maggie up in her woolly creations, I made up a bundle; a few biscuits, a knife and a bottle of water. I then carved some Satanic looking bullshit symbols into the paisley painting work, broke a window or two, kissed them both on the forehead, and took to the deck. The full moon was lost in the willow’s foliage, but its light still slivered the waters and illuminated the bank I was going to have to climb. It wasn't going to be easy. I stood on the bow, considering my route, when the wide beam of a searchlight illuminated the trees two hundred yards downriver. The beam was moving slow but steady, any unexpected sound, such as me scrabbling up the steep bank, was bound to alert the searchers to my presence. But what choice did I have? It was that or get caught onboard and risk Joe and Maggie's safety. I was about to make the jump when I felt the boat rise beneath me, as if it had been hit by a trailing wake. I looked to the water, something huge was stirring in the mud beneath the boat. The water thickened, churned and broke as the blood unicorn rose to the surface, and rested its massive head on the narrowboat's bow.

The creature's gaze was cold and mocking, as calculating as a hunting lion. It knew me as one of its own. I felt its low growl reverberate through the decking and rise through my bones – I had a choice to make, get onboard the beast or take my chances with the advancing searchlight – it was really no choice at all. I stepped onto its head, dropped down onto its mud covered back and wrapped my arms and legs around its massive neck. The creature's bass growl pitched into a bone rattling purr as it pushed itself free of the narrowboat and dived into the cold, crushing, darkness. I gritted my teeth, shut my eyes and dug my fingers deep into its hide, and let the darkness take me.

11

I was shivering, caked in mud, and spitting sludge that tasted like every kind of shit known to man. As I clawed the filth from my eyes, nose and ears, I could feel the thud-thud of the creature's slow stride pass through my body as it turned its huge bulk around and passed over me. I managed to catch a muddied blur of its arse disappearing into a reed swathed swamp and felt the panic of abandonment race through me - and then I saw the lights. A multitude of lights, grey flickering specks moving in twisting, drifting circles through the darkness around the reedy pond. Lone dancers and ghostly couples, all lost in their own circuit of their dance. I was back in the park. I searched through the dancing phantoms for a face I recognised, and I finally found Derek and Harry dancing together, circling the kiddie swings – which made some kind of sense; "you got a minute there Derek?"

Derek was leading and Harry was doing a fine job following his lead. They made a very graceful pair. But both remained silent, seemingly unaware of my presence. I stepped in closer to make sure.

"Derek you pervert. Oi Mr Nonce, you paedo scumbag. Harry you dirty little peeping-tom wank fiend. It's me your killer. Good to see you guys. Any idea what's going on?"

Nothing – not so much as a ripple. I looked into their eyes and saw even less. No matter how hollow their doom was, they were fully absorbed in it. There's no point in flogging a dead perve so I decided to leave them to it, but I couldn't resist a last futile gesture, "I'm sorry Harry. I should never have...." I laid a hand on his shoulder, and the air around me immediately ignited in a flare of white light. I was thrown over the seesaw and landed in a shaking, smoking heap twelve feet from where I started.

Dazed, charged and literally buzzing. Every joint, tooth, pore and hair felt like it had been zapped – lightening will do that. When I finally stopped seeing in triplicate, I saw that I had been encircled by the phantoms, but they weren't dancing anymore, now they were fixed on me, with stares of accusatory silence.

"What the fuck Harry? I was only apologising. I guess I had that coming. And I guess I've got this coming too. Is there any way out of the dance? Or is this like karmic shit? Because I've never been much of a dancer," all of this I've imagined myself saying and wish I'd said, but truth be told; I just crawled through the circle of ghouls and crawled my way to the road that surrounds the park, where, I sat there on the curb – blasted to buggery and feeling it.

A slew of police procedural T.V shows had installed two maxims into my consciousness. Firstly, a criminal will always return to the scene of the crime – check. Secondly, a criminal will always return to the ground he knows best, meaning he will always go home. A fox always returns to its set, isn't that the saying? And I was certainly trying to, but not the 'home' they called my home. I was thinking on a completely different plane. But I was hurting and fading fast. Being caught would have been a mercy, and they were sure to be watching the parents' house, so if I wanted to bring an end to this thing, that was the place to go. But I wasn't ready to give up. I needed to get to that underpass just one more time. I had to give it one more try, even if the outcome was a foregone conclusion. I was resolved; I would get there or die trying. And then I tried to stand up, and everything, including my resolve, crumbled – I was done. I folded into the road and waited for a car to finish the job.

I didn't have long to wait. Three hundred yards away, headlights appeared from around the bend and picked up their pace as they bore down on me. I shut my eyes and waited. Breaks squealed and I heard the cars bodywork judder, and the mass of its presence looming above me. I heard the door open and hurried footsteps.

"You alright there love? Are you hurt?" the silhouette of a tall man stood between me and the night sky.

"I fell over."

"Do you need an ambulance or something?"

"No, I ... I need to get home. Could you drop me off at the Popley underpass?"

"Sure, no problem."

I have never been so grateful. I climbed into the back of a car that I couldn't identify even now, it smelt of bleach and pine disinfectant. I had time to realise that I'd just climbed into the back of a stranger's car – and then I passed out.

12

I was dreaming of bees. A swarm of tiny cleaning bees, happily buzzing around a hive, loaded with tiny mops and dusters, all praising the attributes of beeswax. When suddenly a hot jet of pine disinfectant flooded through their hive and boiled them all alive. I awoke to find myself drowning, my whole body a single flame of pain. Above me; a swinging bucket, rained hot, stinging, pine disinfectant down onto my naked, bruised body. I tried to move out of its reach only to discover my wrists and ankles were tied to what looked like an MFI kitchen table – a very undignified, exposed, and perilous pose.

"And there she is, thanks for joining us," a voice somewhere beyond my head chuckled, "I thought you'd appreciate a quick freshen up. You smelt like a cesspit. I'm going to have to have my car valeted."

I've never felt so vulnerable. It was terrifying, and humiliating, and all I could think to say was, "why am I naked?"

His laugh was derisive, "don't worry. Your virtue is intact. What was I supposed to do? I couldn't leave you in those clothes, they were disgusting and your wounds needed dressing. You really should be thanking me."

"Thanking you! So what's with the water torture?" The bucket was dripping the last of its load onto my stomach.

"Oh that's just for fun."

"Untie me! Untie me right now you fuck!"

"Ummm... no. I think not. You've got some nerve coming back here. Not the smartest move. Some kind of death wish, is it?"

"Untie me and I'll show you a death wish."

"Now that's no way to win my trust Anna, and you do need to win my trust. We are going to need to trust one another, if we're going to get along."

"I'm naked and tied to a table and you want me to trust you? Not a great start! Untie me right now, untie me!"

"No, shan't."

Seized by panic, I thrashed against the tabletop and instantly felt every nerve in my body ignite in protest. The pain startled a single thought into being; "think!" My head was raging with a thrash metal beat that I had to control if I was going to figure a way out. Fight and flight are no use when you're displayed like a spatchcock chicken. It was time to conjure up the good stuff, the wholesome and safe stuff to birth the peace I couldn't feel. But where to look? I went to my cupboard of good memories and the cupboard was bare. No, that's a lie. It was full of dust and rabid rat monsters of my own making. I'd find no comfort there. And then, I felt a desperate longing to be back on that narrowboat with Joe and Maggie, a fresh pain washed over me, as sharp and clean as a scalpel. I heard the sound of lapping water, the click of Maggie's knitting needles, smelt cough sweets and diesel – and felt my pulse drop.

"Who are you? And what do you want with me?"

"That's more like it. Goal orientated I like it."

"Goal orientated," I heard myself laugh and it sounded desperate, "what are you, an occupational therapist? What's next basket weaving? If is this your idea of macrame, I'm not impressed."

"Macrame? What's that then? Something they taught you in the loony bin?"

"So, you know who I am. What do you want with me? Trussing me up like turkey is going to be hard to explain to the authorities."

"True, but I have other plans for you. Would you like to hear them?"

"Sure, why don't you come over here where I can see you, so I can spit in your eye."

Charlie Chaplin appeared above me, in the form of a large plastic mask. I very nearly screamed. Chaplin always gave me the creeps. A bare arm and chest leant across me and applied pressure to my sternum, and then I did scream.

"Nasty wound that, you've popped a couple of stiches. I did the best I could, but I can't guarantee you won't get an infection. You're breathing already sounds a bit bubbly, not a good sign, considering what I've got planned," a well-toned, muscular and very naked Charlie Chaplin stepped into my field of vision.

"Who are you? What do want?" my voice sounded so thin and weak I could have wept for shame.

"Nothing that I can't take," a large and shiny kitchen knife glinted in the fluorescent kitchen strip light, as the hand holding it swept the Charlie Chaplin mask away, to reveal a run-of-the-mill, square jawed, pretty boy, with a malevolent grin, "behold your maker!"

"Not my maker, I am my own creation."

"You don't remember me do you..." he actually sounded offended, and then a firm, broad, hand gripped my jaw and held it firm as his face moved in close, blurring as it pressed into mine, and cold hard lips and a warm searching tongue collided with my clamped mouth. My memory retrieved the sensation, delaying any attempt to bite off the slug of a tongue. The hand released my jaw and I spat in fury, “try that again Lawson, I dare you!”

“So, you do remember me. How’s it going Anna-Conda

“You tell me Paul?”

“Well, it’s not looking good is it. You know I couldn’t believe my luck when I saw you laying in the road. Part of me said, back-up, mow her down, you’ll be hailed as a hero, but the better part of me said no, there’s purpose to the universe if you only look for it. Believe it or not you’ve been on mind ever since your murder spree.”

“And why’s that Paul? Did I kill someone you cared about? I do hope so.”

Paul’s slap set my ears ringing, “don’t be ridiculous, you’d be turning on a spit with my blade up your dirty snatch. No, our link is deeper than that. I’ve read the court transcripts. I know why you did what you did, and for a while there I felt responsible. I felt I owed you an apology. I felt guilt and I haven’t felt that for a very long time. I didn’t like it. But I came to realise that my ... dark predilections were in fact creative acts, and that my acts of desecration, had created you. You owe me, for I am your creator, I made you the monster you are, I made you.”

“What the hell are you talking about? I did what I did because I wanted to, nobody made me do anything, and certainly not you.”

“I made you,” he hissed, “I am your maker. I killed Sally Kent.”

“You? You killed Sally. They nailed Harold Pole for that.”

“Mr Guineapig Man. He went down for it, that’s true, but let’s face it, that old nonce could barely tie his own shoes. They thought he did it because I wanted them to. I’d been watching her for months and months. They’d been a few dry runs before her, experiments really, a refining of my skills. An old lady here, a student nurse. But they were unimportant, it was Sally I wanted. That last week was so charged, watching the two of you together, waiting for an opportunity. And then when I saw her walk into that underpass, I just couldn’t hold back. And then it all went wrong. I wanted to bring her back here, so we could spend some time together, but as soon as I grabbed her, I heard someone approaching, and I knew she’d recognised me so I couldn’t run, I had to kill her. And then it turns out to be Harold Pole, Mr Guineapig Man shuffling his way around the estate looking for dandelions to feed his filthy little rodents. He found her seconds after I killed her. I wasn’t sure if he'd seen me, and I couldn't have him going to the police, I'd barely started my reign of terror. So, I broke into his place and hid the knife in his house. In with those dirty stinking rodents. The police are such idiots."

"You killed horse-faced Sally?" I could hardly believe it, "why? You were Mr Popular, you were going out with that bitch &&&&&, you could have any girl you wanted, why take it out on Sally?"

"Why take what's offered when you can take what you want. Anyway, forbidden fruit is always the sweetest. So, you see, you owe me everything, you owe me, obedience, I am your creator."

I'm sure, at this juncture, I don't need to point out that I'm no psychiatrist, but it was clear to me that Paul Lawson was driving with a wonky driveshaft. That boy had a head full of slugs that needed squishing.

"Tell me Paul, what happens next? How am I supposed to show my obedience?"

"Bow down before me."

"I'm tied to a table Paul."

"You will approach on your knees," Paul's righthand began to work at his less than impressive cock.

"Of course..."

Paul's face reddened, "you will fall down and worship me, taste of my seed and see the righteousness of my path. Join me, and together we shall become a righteous plague upon the world, death and destruction conjoined, we shall burn and bright and beautiful path!"

"What's the matter Paul? Did mummy not love you enough? Or did mummy love you a little too much?" Is what I was thinking but I didn't need another slap, angering him was not wise. Paul was a frayed was a thread away from massacring anyone who crossed his path – and I didn't want to be first in line, "is there any chance we could start with my parents?"

"Of course, I am your true parent. I am your creator. Obey me, and together, we will ravage the world. Frankenstein and his creature. We shall become gods. Legends of terror!" The kitchen knife glinted above me, "do you swear to obey me! Do you swear your allegiance my creature?"

"I do," my bonds were cut.

"On your knee's creature, honour your creator! And there he stood, knife in one hand, held aloft like some mini-

Excalibur, whilst his other hand presented his perky little mini pecker, waiting to be worshipped.

I dropped from the table and onto my knees before him, but couldn't help but laugh, "Paul, did you ever read Frankenstein?"

He looked down at me and grinned, "I saw the movie. The Hammer Horror version."

"That makes sense," I grabbed his balls and twisted. The knife was thrust down into my shoulder; it glanced off the bone but hurt like fuck. Luckily, for me, he'd hacked into the wrong arm. I tightened my grip and twisted with all my might. The knife lunged down wildly, ripping through my ear, but it moved with such force, that the stroke followed through, and sunk into Paul's thigh. He staggered backwards yanking the blade from his flesh. His blood poured from the wound, pumping with a regular beat, something vital had been severed. Paul's face was a picture of shock and disbelief, as if someone had just crushed his favourite toy trainset engine. Lawson launched himself forward, his hands locked around my throat as his weight pressed down upon me. I pushed my bloodied fingers hard into his ears. If you think that doesn't hurt, try it. His gripped tightened, I could feel his fingertips gouching my windpipe, as his weight crushed the air from my body. I felt like was being squeezed out of existence, popped like a snail on a stone anvil. And then he suddenly pushed himself clear and scrabbled across the bloodied floor, until his back was against the blood splattered cooker. There was a crimson river between us, and none of it was mine. I saw the light of realisation flash across his face – and disappear into nothingness.

Slowly, I eased myself up, out of the bloody mess and steadied myself on the MFI marble effect kitchen worktop, feeling how close I'd come to never moving again in every aching inch. I then lifted a heavy wooden chopping board from its hanger above the aluminium breadbin and beat Lawson's head until it split in two. And when it was done, I beat him some more. And when I was done with that, you could have collected what was left in a bucket... which I would have pissed in if it had been there.

I went upstairs to find some clothes. I don't know who decorated Lawson place, but the décor certainly expressed the personality of the occupant. The Borgias meets Himmler meets the House of Usher, but with less finesse. There was, of course, an Ed Gein inspired room, adorned with atrocities that made me want to revive the fucker and feed him back through a meatgrinder, but alas the devil was never going to relinquish his hold on that soul. I had half a mind to go back to the park and see if the evil fucker could be roused to a rematch – and then I thought, fuck him, he's done.

I sat on Lawson's bed – the room was all straight lines and hard edges. Black and white geometric thick pile rug, white walls and sleek white closets edged with black metal, all finished off with bright red sliding blinds. All very cold and calculating. The most alive think in the room was the bedsheets, they hadn't been changed in weeks, skanky boy. There were three wrist watches sitting on his bedside table. I picked up a digital Seiko, it looked like a cross between a watch, a calculator and a gas metre, very manly – it was five thirty p.m. I had time to kill. I thought about having a shower, but when I saw the lifeless schoolgirl in the shower, I decided to give it a miss. I bound my wounds using four of Lawson's very smart C&A shirts. Then made a cup of tea and sat down on the bed to watch some tele. Of course, Lawson owned a ridiculously large television set, and a highly questionable video collection, which seemed to rotate around Japanese school girls, Enema Erotica and Arsenal Football Club – I really had done the world a favour. The lead story on the local news, continued to be the so-called drama of my escape and my seemingly miraculous disappearance, and the whole, "Do not approach, alert the police at once," stance, which I found slightly insulting. It's not like I'm a maniac or something, I didn't cut people up in my kitchen and sew them into my furniture. Peeved but knackered I switched over to a gameshow and instantly wanted to kill the smiling host and his brainless contestants, so I switched to a BBC history program and instantly fell asleep.

It was dark when I woke up. I almost panicked, I checked the ridiculous watch – it said it was 11:25. Plenty of time – and then I realised that I didn't know where I was, I'd just assumed I was still in Popley. I could be miles from the underpass – and I had to get there for midnight if I was in for the slightest chance of meeting myself coming back. I turned the place over, found a letter with an address that indicated I was on the Oakridge estate, but I needed to be sure, so I called up the BT operator; "Hello operator, I know this is going to sound strange, but could you tell me where I'm calling from?" Oakridge it was – I was a brisk ten-minute walk from the underpass. One last push and then... one way or another, I was going to end the nightmare.

13

It was five minutes to midnight when I stepped into the familiar stink of the underpass. The walls had been painted and the lights repaired, but the stink remained the same. But of course, there was nobody there. Hope sank, even though I really hadn't expected anything else. I felt as hollow as that tunnel and twice as dark. It was time to round up the horror show I called my life, and join the dancers in the park, I could endure no more. You may think it dramatic but the first thing I did was throw that ridiculous watch against the underpass' wall.

"Temper, temper," my voice echoed down the tunnel towards me.

And there I was, walking towards me.

"Bitch, where the fuck have you been?" I leant against the wall and waited for myself to approach.

"Are you hurt?"

"Yes, I'm hurt, you fucking arsehole. Have you any idea what I've been through?"

"I'm sorry. I know what we agreed…"

"Six hours! Guess what, you're late! By six months!"

"I'm sorry. I just wanted to see Sally again, and when I did, I just couldn't leave her..."

"But you left me with kissy-kissy Slightly, thanks very much!"

"You really shouldn't call him that, he doesn't like it. His names Simon."

"Fuck you."

"Wouldn't that be masturbation," she dared to grin.

"Would kicking you in the head be self-harm?"

"Sorry, you look dreadful. What happened?"

"I met Sally's killer. Don't worry, he won't be bothering you again."

The face before me paled, "I thought he was in prison."

"What? Not him... look, don't worry about it. It's sorted that's all you need to know."

The colour returned to her face, "sorted... okay. How's Simon?"

"How's Simon? I don't believe you, how's Simon? I just told you I've... about Sally's murderer and you want to know how Simon is?"

"You told me it was sorted."

"You need to address your communication skills!"

My face sneered back at me, "you didn't tell me my Mum was dead. And you didn't tell me about Dad's drinking."

I answered with a shrug, "yeah, okay so we both need to work on our communication skills," the stoney look I was receiving from myself was working, "okay, look the truth is, I don't even remember my mum… so yeah I wanted to spend some time with her."

"I understand. How is she?"

"Mum? Grand, you know Mum, fit as a fiddle. You're very lucky, and now you know how lucky you are, which means you can appreciate it."

"I always appreciated her, always."

And I believed her, "well now you can appreciate it even more. How's my dad?"

"Your Dad died last week, I'm sorry. He wasn't a well man. I was with him at the end."

And there I was crying. I slumped to the pavement and wept, “sorry, I don’t know what that was. I didn’t even like him.”

“Who you kidding? He was your dad,” her hand fell on my shoulder, as she knelt down beside me and I hugged myself.

“It does feel I bit like masturbation,” I sniffed.

“Idiot,” she sniffed, “listen, I don’t want to go back, not for good. But losing your dad, was hard. I want to see my parents. I miss my Mum. I just want to see them one last time and then, I want to go back to Sally. Do you mind staying here?”

“With Mum and Dad... no, of course not,” I grinned, and I really meant it.

“Just one last time. Just for a few hours, a day at most. But I must come back for Sally.”

“Not a problem for me but how can I trust you? What if you decide to stay?”

“I won’t I promise. And you’ve got to promise too.”

“And I give you, my word. I’ll be back tomorrow. Do I have to see Sally?”

"Good god no, she's away with her sister for the weekend."

"Sister, I didn't know she had a sister? Okay, let's do it. Back her midnight tomorrow and no later."

"Agreed."

I hobbled towards the Popley end using the wall as a support, whilst she marched towards the Oakridge end.

"Are you sure you're alright?"

"I can honestly say I've never felt better, but do me a favour, when you see Mum, give her a hug from me."

"That I can promise. After three, one, two, three…"

I stepped out of the tunnel and there sat a bright red Ford Fiesta, with its headlights illuminating the path into Popley.

"Anna-Conda I presume," a voice called from the driver's seat.

"Slightly, when did you learn to drive?"

"It is you!" and suddenly I was being embraced in the front of a Ford Fiesta, "God it's so good to see you. She was so dull. You have no idea."

“So, she told you then?”

“Oh, I knew something was up from the very start. Not a nipple twist in weeks, it was weird and very, very dull. She confessed everything, her mum this, her dad that, God she was so dull. How you doing?”

“Well let’s see... I’ve travelled to a parallel world, been locked up, stabbed, chased by religious fanatics, stabbed again... and I’ve talked with the dead. How’s that for starters? Take me home Slater, take me home and patch me up.”

The car did not move, “I need to tell you something,” Slater cringed.

“My dad died. She told me.”

“Not that.”

“She made you promise to bring me back here at midnight.”

“True, but not that...”

I reached over, and gave Slightly’s nipple a gentle tweak, he shuddered, “I missed you Slightly.”

“Anna, I’m trying to tell you about Sally!”

"Don't shout, I'm getting a headache."

"You need to heat this..."

"I know, she's alive and we're an item, I get it,"

"Sally has a baby. That Paul Lawson's the father, if you can believe that!"

"Bitch!"

The car pulled away as smoothly as a kiss.

14

I ache all over and my head is killing me. The minute I stepped into that car it kicked in, and it hasn't stopped since. The funeral didn't help, it was dire, so dull. All Dad's so called 'friends from work,' turned up to eat the cold buffet, that I didn't know that I'd organised – arseholes to the lot of them. Luckily, they mistook my headache for grief and pretty much let me be, but I was hugged, forcibly mothered by middle-aged women, and that's never a good thing. Dad left me the house, and a pension policy that should help me out for a while once the paperwork goes through. Slightly's moving in next week, we'll see how long that lasts. He's sitting on the sofa right now, filling his face with crisps, watching Hello Dolly again, dressed in leather chaps and a white t-shirt that reads, Frankie Says Relax.

Sally came home a few days ago, which was both awkward and amusing. What amused me was how little she questioned my sudden weight loss, change of hairstyle, accumulated injuries and general battered appearance. People will believe anything you tell them, as long as it benefits them to do so. The awkward element was of course the child, a little girl as it turns out, Thelma. She's really going to thank her mother for that one. I think Sally said she was three months old. She's yet to take on her mother's distinctive features, but I can certainly see her father in there. Perhaps it's too early to determine if she carries any of her father's other foibles, and it will certainly be too late to do anything about it by the time one can be sure of such things. Perhaps I should break up with Sally. Give the kid some space. Give it a chance to grow without my malign influence. And then again, if the apple does turn sour, who better to do what needs to be done than me? The thing is, I'm also considering not breaking up with Sally. Simon told me, that Sally told me that the thing with Simon was basically rape. A drunken night she doesn't remember consenting to, and remembers nothing about – having seen Paul's member, I can believe that. I would visit Paul and see what he can be induced to recall, but Slightly tells me I've promised not to, we shall see. Anyway, I like Sally, she's a lot of fun and we do have a sort of history between us and looks aren't everything... and I don't dislike horses.

On reflection, I think Paul is safe as long as he doesn't give Sally a hard time. My darker appetites seem to have been appeased, and although I know you can never say, never again, I do feel as if something inside has switched off... or perhaps on? If the beast still roams the estate, it seems to be giving me a wide berth, and to be honest, if it did turn up again, I'm certain I wouldn't follow it back to that underpass. It's impossible to know if dancing in the park is still in my future or not. But it's also impossible to know what's going to happen next week. Will I be diagnosed with some incurable disease? Will a speeding pensioner wipe me out of existence? Will I have to do something about that baby and then spend the rest of my life in prison? Perhaps I can escape the park by leading a good life from here on out, or perhaps doing what needs to be done, protecting the future from future harm, will ensure my escape? I could become some kind of negative saint, beatified by what I chose not to do, or what I choice not to let happen. I see those dancers in the park and wonder if I'm already there, forever condemned to prance about with the perves, forever waltzing with Derek and Harry. I don't know, my confidence in time and the hitch-free nature of the universe has been undermined of late.

It makes my head hurt thinking about it. And my head's already thumping. It feels as if someone's hit me other the head with a bottle and not quite finished the job. And I've got a strange taste in my mouth, it's a sickly bittersweet... Liebfraumilch, why can I taste Liebfraumilch? Okay enough already, this isn't helping my head. I'm going to bed and see what dreams may come.

www.ingramcontent.com/pod-product-compliance
Lightning Source LLC
LaVergne TN
LVHW091135080826
845145LV00008B/2163